CROSSROADS

A Novel

Maya Lippman

Bind International, LLC

ISBN: 979-8-9897608-0-0

eISBN: 979-8-9897608-1-7

Book Cover by M. Lippman

First Edition 2024

Prologue

She laid out the short black dress that she would wear to the funeral. As she began to zip it up, she thought about how much he loved to watch her dress. And especially how he loved to watch her undress. He was very clear about what he liked, and definitely what he disliked. He would even buy her clothes, and made sure he saw her wearing them, or she would never hear the end of it.

Carefully following the outline of her lips, she put on her bright red lipstick. She then wondered what he would be wearing in the casket. A black suit? He always looked good in black. A navy pinstripe? No, too conservative. Then she smiled. She remembered that he always wanted to be cremated. Good, burn in hell!

She then slipped on her black stiletto heels. Too high for a funeral? No, that was just the way he liked them.

Chapter One

The funeral for Jake Baines was at Riverside Memorial on 76th Street and Amsterdam Avenue.

Cara stepped out of the black car, extending her hand for her mother. A man from Riverside greeted them at the door and showed them in. The Jake Baines funeral would be upstairs in one of the gathering rooms.

The photo of Jake on the easel by the door was taken many years ago when he was younger and slim. He had gotten fuller around the middle, with gray hair sprinkled about, but the eyes never changed. They were intense blue eyes. Connie looked at the photo and shook her head. Jake was forty-six years old.

Cara ushered her mother inside. Both women had shoulder length red hair and they were hard to miss. Behind them, a well-dressed couple in their sixties arrived. The man said he worked with Jake in advertising many years ago, and he was sorry they had not stayed in touch. Connie nodded and smiled. Cara said nothing. Connie's friends arrived, hugged Connie and Cara, and then took seats in the back to leave the front rows for family. The family members from Albany joined them in the front row. A man named Luke who used to work with Jake came in with his wife, offered condolences to Connie, then took seats several rows behind them on the aisle.

Cara looked around. There were women who came alone. Maybe some of them were Jake's former girlfriends. Jake always had girlfriends, but never married. Cara wondered how many hearts he had broken. How many of these women had imagined a life with Jake Baines, the happy, handsome, advertising executive? Had they seen themselves in a house with children, expensive cars, and a future filled with joy with this man?

There was no casket. Only an urn filled with Jake's ashes perched on a pedestal at the front of the room. How strange, Cara thought, that a life can be reduced to what could be a bag of flour.

Finally, everyone took a seat. The man from the funeral home went to the podium that had been placed behind the urn, welcomed everyone and then said that we were all here to remember the life of a fine man, Jake Baines. He had obviously never met Jake. He then invited Jake's sister Connie to come to the podium.

Connie had a hard time speaking. She said some words about how much Jake meant to her, and then pulled out a piece of paper with a poem hand-written on it called *Afterglow*.

He'd like the memory of him to be a happy one.
He'd like to leave an afterglow of smiles when life is done.
He'd like to leave an echo whispering softly down the ways,
Of happy times, laughing times and bright and sunny days.
He'd like the tears of those who grieve, to dry before the sun;
Of happy memories that he leaves when life is done.

When Connie finished, she returned to her seat. No one else rose to speak.

Chapter Two

When Cara remembered her childhood, it was always the summertime. Hot sticky summers in the city when the sidewalk heat seeped into her Keds and warmed her feet.

She grew up on the upper, Upper West Side of Manhattan near Columbia University. Back in the early 1960s, saying she lived by Columbia University was simply to obscure the fact that her neighborhood was scary. She was warned it was dangerous to go to the lower 100s, or even 90s, and God forbid going north. And don't go east past Amsterdam Avenue. To the west was Riverside Park, considered especially dangerous for a kid. There were so many "don'ts" growing up on the Upper West Side of Manhattan then. As Cara got older, she became ashamed of living on 115th Street.

Cara was the only child of Mel Jacob and Connie Baines. Connie was a jewelry designer, and grew up in the Chelsea neighborhood. She was ninety-five pounds petite, with a fiery temper that occasionally flared and red hair to match. Cara got her red hair from her. Connie was also "earthy" which meant she never wore makeup, never got her nails done, and cooked a lot. In general, she was tough, and expected her daughter to be tough too.

Her father Mel was from Albany, and moved to New York City to attend Columbia University as a history major, and where he later became a professor specializing in Renaissance Art. He was warm, affectionate and understanding, and the person Cara went to on those bad days when she felt sad. Mel used to say he loved living across from Columbia because nobody grew old. Maybe he wished it would rub off on him. He was otherwise oblivious to how sketchy the neighborhood was, and even though the apartment was small, it was cheap. One hundred and fifty-six dollars a month, and that was cheap even in 1965. The apartment building was owned by Columbia University, but their apartment was rent controlled so they could be there forever if they wanted.

Then there was Cara's Uncle Jake, Connie's brother, who lived about fifteen blocks away on 98th Street. Jake was a slim six-footer, with brown wavy hair, expressive blue eyes and an infectious smile. He lit up a room when he entered.

"Where's the little Munchkin who lives in this house?" he'd yell out when he came to visit. Cara would run and hide and before Jake would take his jacket off, he'd be peeking behind doors and crouching under tables until there were giggles and then laughter as he found her. She adored her tall, funny, huggable uncle.

Despite the safety issues of the neighborhood, Cara's parents worked hard to instill in her a sense of independence. To feel strong no matter what things looked like. To that end, they provided her with the necessary tools all children in New York City needed to know:

"Don't talk to strangers"

"Never get into a strange car with someone you don't know"

"Never accept candy from anyone outside our home"

"Always have your key out when you come home so you are ready to open the door"

"Never let someone in the front door behind you unless you know them".

Cara was always aware and prepared.

Actually, these warnings came in handy when Cara was six and her best friend Ginny, who lived on the ninth floor, were waiting on the front steps for Connie to take them food shopping.

A man approached and said that his car had broken down and asked if there was a place where he could change from his work clothes to casual ones so he could repair his car. Cara thought, this is the stranger her parents had warned her about. She refused to answer his question. Ginny however proceeded to tell him that maybe there was a room in the basement he could use or perhaps if the laundry room was empty, he could change there. The man perked up and asked if she could take him to show him where this was. Ginny started to say something when Cara cut her off and said "my mother is on her way down to take us shopping" and glared at him. The man tried again saying that all she needed was to quickly show him the basement. Cara firmly said "no". He looked at the girls, smiled then left. Cara had felt threatened, but then Ginny asked Cara why she was so rude to the man?

When Cara's mother came to get them, Cara told her what had just happened and Connie said, "Cara, that was good. You handled that well."

Ginny and Cara were inseparable. They liked the same things and even dressed alike. They both wore dresses with flowers and Mary Janes with white socks, and both wore their hair in pigtails. Sometimes they pretended they were twins even though Cara was tiny with red hair and Ginny was tall with brown hair.

Cara and Ginny had been friends since they were toddlers, introduced at a Music Land playgroup on West End Avenue. Ginny loved music and Cara loved art. Cara could sit for hours on her bed with her drawing pad. It went everywhere with her and she practiced first with crayons, then pencils, and then watercolor. Both girls attended St. Hilda's and St. Hugh's Elementary School, which was an Episcopal day school in the neighborhood. It was inexpensive, and for a lot of parents at that time it was a blessing.

The Jacob family was neither Episcopalian nor religious at all for that matter. Mel Jacob was a non-practicing Jew and Connie was a non-practicing Catholic. So little Cara Jacob going to St. Hilda's and St. Hugh's was the butt of many jokes at family gatherings. The school's teachers were mostly nuns and some were good, and some were a bit odd. Cara told her parents that one nun came to class every day, sat down at her desk, cried softly for about thirty seconds, then composed herself and proceeded to teach the class. Another nun told them that sexual feelings were normal and that they shouldn't feel bad if they had them. This was to five- and six-year olds, and it was supposed to be a spelling class. Cara knew when odd was odd. Ginny was more naïve. She would worry about the nun who cried every morning, wondering if there was something she could do to make her feel better. Cara told her, "I don't think you can do anything. It's just the way she is, and she's a bit strange."

Chapter Three

Ginny was five and stayed in her room, the room she shared with her older sister, Sara. Her parents, Barbara and Peter, were fighting again. She tried to concentrate on her reading, and then, after an hour or so, decided to build a Lego house. She concentrated hard to make a pattern around the walls of her house, carefully choosing the red and white bricks in an alternating pattern creating a checkerboard wall. She tried her best to block out the yelling of her father. She never heard her mother say anything, only her father's voice in these fights. After she built the Lego walls, she created the roof with the green flat Legos. After the roof was secured, she realized that her house had no windows. If anyone were to live in this house it would be a jail. Then she turned the house around and saw there was no door either, so it couldn't be a jail. It was a tomb.

After the fights her father Peter would storm out of the apartment and walk the neighborhood for an hour or so.

Barbara stayed behind and sat in the kitchen staring off into space. Ginny never knew what the fights were about, she just knew she felt scared. She would go home with Cara after school and stay there until dinner time. She never wanted to go home. Some nights she was invited to stay for dinner and stayed until bedtime. Since they lived in the same building, that was easy for her to do.

Connie knew why Ginny wanted to stay. She never shared it with Cara, but she felt sorry for Ginny. Ginny was so young, and shy. Her sister Sara, who was nine years older, went out a lot now with friends to escape. Ginny looked up to Cara whom she saw as much stronger and confident.

Mel and Connie frequently invited Ginny to their country home by Lake George in the summer where Cara and Ginny would share a room and have sleepovers. These were special times, when Mel would take the girls on hikes and to Calves Pen to watch people jumping off the cliffs. Ginny and Cara wanted to jump, but Mel told them they were too young, even when they were in their teens. Cara teased Mel, telling him that she'd never grow up in his eyes. He agreed.

Then there were the visits to Lake George from Cara's Uncle Jake, who was always fun and took the girls for ice cream, and in their boat on the lake. He taught them how to play backgammon, parcheesi and chess. He also set up poles and a net on the back lawn so they could play badminton. Cara adored her Uncle Jake as did Ginny.

Ginny loved her summers with Cara's family and dreaded going back home.

One day when Ginny was six, she was out with Sara and her mother and when they came home there was a chair placed in the hallway with an envelope on it. Her mother opened the envelope, read the letter and stood there stunned.

"Your father has moved out," she said.

Sara said nothing and went to her bedroom. Cara ran to her mother to hug her and cried. She quietly asked if there was a note for her. Her mother shook her head.

She watched as her mother called her father begging him to come home crying. She couldn't make sense of that since he was always yelling at her when he was home. Ginny remembers the day that her father Peter took Sara and Ginny out for lunch at a diner nearby and told them that he was moving to Chicago. Sara looked away when he said that. Ginny asked if he would be coming to see them or if they could visit him. He said probably, but he'd let them know.

One day at school Ginny and her classmates were given recorders to practice playing. She liked creating music. Because she was good at the recorder, they offered her a flute to try. She loved it.

Creating music was her escape after her father left. Her mother was not emotionally available. Ginny stayed in her room when she was home, either listening to her records or playing her flute.

Chapter Four

Mel stood near the front door waiting. Cara was in her room putting on the fluffy pink dress Mel's brother had sent for her seventh birthday. Cara heard her mother through her bedroom door saying the dress was gaudy and tacky. She could hear Mel trying to shush her. He had seen how Cara's face had lit up when she opened the box. It was a soft pink dress with short puffy sleeves and a full skirt with crinoline underneath so the skirt looked like something a ballerina would wear, which was why Cara loved it. She was crushed to hear her mother's comments.

But then Mel told Cara, he'd like to take her out, and she should wear that dress. He'd be proud to walk with her. Cara was so happy. She ran to put it on.

One of their favorite things to do together was visit the Barnard college campus and watch the tennis players. Barnard had two outdoor tennis courts on its small campus.

They'd sit on the benches in front of the courts and watch the games. Mel played ping pong, he would say, but never mastered tennis. He used to joke with Cara saying that he was good at the little things in life. After watching the games, they would stroll down Broadway to their favorite ice cream parlor, where she always ordered chocolate chip ice cream with chocolate sprinkles.

That day walking down Broadway in her new pink dress holding her father's hand, Cara felt like a princess. She loved her time with Mel. He would ask her opinions, and include her in their decisions of what to do. He listened well, and never interrupted her, as her mother did. As she grew older, he took her to museums because he knew she loved to draw and paint. He pointed out the different styles of art too. Mel loved Impressionist art and Cara loved the Surreal artists, such as Salvador Dali. Her favorite painting by Dali was his dripping clocks called The Persistence of Memory. She had seen it at the Museum of Modern Art. Mel made sure to buy her a poster of it so she could put it on the wall in her room.

Chapter Five

"C'mon Jake you can do it! Jump!" Connie yelled. Jake stood at the edge of the ridge. It was about twenty feet down to the water at Calves Pen on Lake George. He felt silly being so scared. He was aware of the other kids laughing at him. He even heard one say that he would make a tidal wave when he went into the water because of his weight. Jake trusted Connie completely. So if she said it was safe to jump, it was. He felt that his heart was beating so hard that everyone must be able to hear it. He took three deep breaths then...in he went. When he surfaced all was good. He scurried up the sides of the rocks and waited for his turn with other kids to jump again.

Connie was six years older than Jake and had always been protective of her little brother. She would move the family cat to another room when he was in a bassinet for fear the cat might scratch him. When Jake was a child, he became overweight and pudgy. He was teased, and would come home upset many times. It became even worse when puberty arrived and his skin broke out. There were times he didn't want to go to school. Instead of becoming shy, he became angry. Sometimes he threw things against the walls in his room. Connie would talk to him, to calm him down. She told him how smart he was, that he had many talents, and that he would grow up to be a handsome man. She did her best to boost his self-esteem.

As Jake grew older and taller, his body became slim and his face cleared up. His confidence grew, he started to feel better about himself and he buried his anger. Being liked by his peers was new to him. Now, people meeting Jake thought he was great, someone who made people feel good. This continued, and as he grew older, his friends saw that he loved to be liked. He needed it. He would say to friends when parting, "I'll call you next week" and "let's have lunch soon" and "we definitely have to do that thing you spoke about". Mostly it never happened. His friends did the follow-up or it never happened. Because Jake always wanted to be the nice guy, he couldn't say no, and often wound up with two plans for the same day. In the end, he canceled the less desirable plan at the last minute, apologizing and saying, "I'll call you next week to reschedule". It became frustrating dealing with him, but friends put up with it because he could turn on the charm. His charisma could be infectious, but it was fake. Connie chided him about his insincerity. "This is going to catch up with you. You can't make promises you know you won't keep." It didn't matter. Jake shook it off. People seemed happy to be with him.

Jake went to Columbia University and then earned his MBA there as well. He decided on a career in Manhattan's advertising world because he kept hearing it was exciting. His first job was an associate at Wieden and Kennedy. Then he moved to Ammirati and Puris, working on Club Med campaigns. After five years, Benton & Bowles recruited him as an executive. He thrived. He loved entertaining clients. Proctor and Gamble and EF Hutton were the most fun. There were private boat rides around Manhattan, dinners at Le Cirque and lavish parties at the New York apartments of high-level executives. Some male clients also expected late evening entertainment with ladies to be provided. They all joined his Rolodex.

One evening, after several months at B & B, Jake noticed a young woman waiting for the elevator. He had seen her before, but never felt the timing was right. "Work here often?" he asked.

"Really? C'mon you can do better than that!"

They both laughed. She brushed her dark hair back and said, "My name is Amanda Swift. I've been here almost a year, but I've never seen you before. Did you just start?"

"Nice to meet you Amanda. I'm Jake Baines. I've been here about six months, so I guess I'm the newby."

The elevator arrived. As they descended, he said, "Listen, you may not have seen me, but I've noticed you. Can I take you to dinner one night?"

Amanda looked surprised, but smiled, "You like to cut to the chase."

They started dating after that.

Chapter Six

Cara and Ginny headed to 137th Street and St. Nicholas Terrace at nine in the morning. They made sure to travel together because they were going to the forbidden territory of "uptown". They took the Broadway local train, then walked. The streets were crowded with people starting their day. There was a happy spirit in the streets. A little boy skipped, holding his mother's hand. A young couple kissed goodbye in front of the subway entrance. Young girls gathered outside a bodega, giggling. It was not the scary world they heard about from their parents. They walked past City College buildings before they saw the beautiful gothic revival building known as The Castle on the Hill.

They entered the arched wooden door of Music and Art High School, then walked up the steep steps to the lobby. They were both nervous and excited to take the entrance exam. Cara carried her portfolio and Ginny brought her flute. Cara joined the line for art applicants and Ginny the music application line. They wished each other good luck and went to their separate test rooms.

Cara walked into a crowded room and was told to wait in another line. She looked around and wondered how many people in this room were going to be accepted. She couldn't wait to be out of St. Hilda's and St. Hugh's. Going to chapel every day with all the nuns was now getting to her. It was 1971. She was thirteen and very skinny. Her school uniform that was ordered always arrived too short because it was based on her waist size. The nuns forced her to rip out the hem to lengthen it so her knees would be covered.

"Name?" asked the man with gray hair and glasses.

"Cara Jacob," she replied.

"Nice to meet you. Ok let's take a look at your work." the man said, and opened her portfolio on the table.

Inside were drawings of a couple on a park bench in Central Park done in pen and ink, some pencil sketches of hands and feet, pastels of lilies in a vase, and a watercolor of a field with dandelions with a dog jumping in the background.

"Excellent pieces using the different mediums," the man said, putting her artwork back in her portfolio. He made some notes. "Now please take a seat around the table over there," he said, pointing behind him.

The table was actually many tables placed in a rectangle around a small circular table with an arrangement of plastic fruit in a bowl. Cara sat down and was handed a sheet of art paper, a drawing pencil and a large pink eraser. She was calmer than she thought she would be. Many other boys and girls took their seats. She waited. After ten minutes, a woman walked to a corner of the rectangle, told the applicants to put their name at the bottom right of the paper, and then to begin. They were given two hours to complete their sketch, but if finished early, could leave. They would be notified of their acceptance in three to four weeks.

After an hour Cara looked at her work. She felt satisfied but looked around to see the other kids still working. She added a few more marks, then told herself, this is ridiculous. She put her pencil down, gathered her portfolio and left the room.

Cara waited in the school lobby for Ginny.

After a half hour, Ginny arrived with a big smile. "Did it go well?" she asked.

"I left early so I hope my test picture was ok. I'm kinda nervous now," Cara said.

"Oh I'm sure you did great. Don't worry. I felt really great with my audition. We'll both be coming here in the fall!" Ginny said excitedly.

Chapter Seven

It was Saturday, mid-March in 1971, and Amanda was running late to meet Jake at Janssen's Restaurant on East 44th. In the winter, the subways were erratic, as was the crosstown bus. Jake told her that he would meet her at Janssen's because his buddy Luke wanted to talk to him about a new woman he started seeing last month. Janssen's was dimly lit, and she had a hard time finding Jake. Finally, she saw him in a corner. He was laughing with Luke and two friends from work and one of their girlfriends, but he stood up when he saw her approaching the table. The friends spoke about business. The other woman was too far away for Amanda to engage, so Amanda joined the B & B conversation. She knew she would probably never see her again.

After dinner Jake and Amanda took a cab downtown to where Amanda lived. They had been dating for about a year now, and spoke about moving in together. Amanda was happy with Jake, and thought about a future with him. His moving in would be a huge step for both of them. She also loved Jake's family, especially Connie, his sister.

Jake and Amanda were planning a vacation to the island of St. John in a week and she couldn't wait. She felt butterflies when she thought about it because she was sure he was going to pop the question. They had talked about the trip for months. Jake rented a place by Caneel Bay where they could take romantic walks along the sandy beach and even have dinner right by the water's edge.

She loved when Jake took her face in his hands, looked into her eyes and told her how much he loved her.

They made love and held each other tightly that night. Sunday morning, they woke up late and planned a fabulous breakfast that they would have in bed. As they were cooking breakfast, the telephone rang. It was Luke. He called at the respectable time of eleven on Sunday morning, but Amanda felt it was an intrusion.

Jake answered the phone and she heard him say "Of course, that would be great! What's her name? Fantastic! Will we get a chance to meet her beforehand? Ok I'll tell Mandy"

Amanda wondered what the call was about.

"Sweetheart, listen, Luke started seeing this girl Anna and he wanted to take her on a vacation. I told him we were going to St. John and he asked if he could join us" Jake said after he had hung up.

"What did you say?" she asked, knowing the answer.

"Luke is a good friend and he wanted to have us meet his new girlfriend so I thought they could join us in St. John," he answered.

"Well, I wished you would have asked me, but I guess it's fine," Amanda replied, but she was not pleased.

Why didn't Jake give her the courtesy to ask her if it was okay, instead of just telling her? They had breakfast and watched an old movie on TV and then Jake went home. Amanda felt uneasy. Why would Jake be so willing to invite a friend on a vacation? She knew he was always a good friend who helped his buddies any time they needed him, but this? When she thought about it, Jake was actually the one always making the social plans. She had her own friends that she saw for girls' lunches and occasional dinners, but anything with Jake and her, he planned. Was she one of those women disappearing in a relationship? She decided to laugh it off. Besides she loved Jake and she liked Luke enough and maybe she'd like Anne or Anna, whatever. She called Jake that night with a cheery voice and blew a kiss into the phone when they said good night.

The day arrived for them to go on their vacation. The four of them met at the airport to board the Pan Am flight to St. Thomas. When they arrived, they took the taxi to the Red Hook Ferry terminal, ferried to St. John, then shared a taxi to Gallows Point, to the Cottage Colony rentals.

The weather was warm with a slight breeze the whole week. They had rented a Jeep to drive around the island seeing the little towns, the occasional wild donkey or goats and the incredible beaches. They visited Denis Bay, Francis Bay, Jumbie Bay, Honeymoon Beach and Amanda's favorite, Solomon Beach. Amanda loved this beach because it was so secluded. Mangrove trees grew close to the water's edge. They had to walk in the water at some points along the beach to get around the mangroves. Amanda and Jake walked ahead of Luke and Anna that day holding hands on the Lind Point Trail that led to the softest white sand she'd ever seen. She waded into the water and was surprised how warm it was. They both lay down on the sand and stared at the few clouds in the blue sky saying nothing. It was so peaceful.

Then, "Guys, isn't this just so gorgeous!" Luke said as he and Anna approached them.

"It's incredible, just like paradise. Come sit with us," Jake said. They stayed a while, swam in the water, then headed back to the guest cottages to get ready for dinner.

The last night in St. John they were all going to have dinner at The Kite overlooking Trunk Bay. The ride was bumpy in their rented Jeep that seemed to lack shock absorbers. The Kite was a small restaurant with delicious simply grilled food. It was foggy by the water's edge where they were sitting and it made the air misty. Amanda felt glum. The trip was okay, but not the dream vacation she had envisioned for so long. She and Jake had had no time to themselves except in their room, which wasn't exactly steaming up with passion this week. That this was the vacation Jake would propose didn't happen, but somehow she wasn't really disappointed about that now. It was their first trip together, and they weren't truly together. She wasn't even sure how to voice this to Jake without seeming selfish and needy.

The following morning, they all met for breakfast and then headed with their packed bags to Cruz Bay to board the ferry back to St. Thomas and then the flight home.

At the exit door at Kennedy Airport in New York Luke and Anna hugged Amanda and Jake promising to see each other again soon. Jake and Amanda shared a taxi to their separate apartments. They both said they were tired from the flight and they kissed good night. Jake walked Amanda to her building's front door, then continued uptown in the taxi. When home, Amanda settled in, unpacked, made herbal tea and curled up on her couch to catch up on mail. She started to feel badly about her feelings for the trip. Okay, so what's the big deal, it was fun. So what if friends joined them, so what if they didn't have a day to themselves? There would be other trips and other days. At eleven, before turning out her light, Amanda dialed Jake's number to say good night. The phone just rang and rang.

Chapter Eight

Cara waited for the mail that Saturday. Nothing came. She called Ginny. She didn't hear anything either. It was four weeks since they had taken the Music and Art entrance exam. They decided to distract themselves by playing handball in the courtyard behind their building. Running after a ball and smacking it against a concrete wall was perfect for the two of them to release the stress. After about an hour they went to Cara's to hang out in her room. Her Uncle Jake had come over to spend time with Connie and Mel. When Jake saw Cara and Ginny he said "You both look down in the dumps. What's going on?"

Connie answered, "They're both waiting for the result of their high school applications. It's been a while."

Jake made a little pouting face and said "Well...why don't I cheer you both up and let's go see a movie? *Harold and Maude* is playing at the Thalia."

Cara and Ginny looked at each other.

"Maybe, I guess..." Cara said.

"Okay then, it's a go. Let me check the showtimes." He opened the New York Times to the movie schedules.

"There's a 2:30 showing and we can just make it," he told them.

"Don't keep the girls out too late, I'm making a pot roast tonight. Ginny, are you staying for dinner?" Connie asked.

"Yes. Thank you," Ginny answered.

"Listen, I'm not gonna join you tonight. I've got a date. Taking her to Trader Vic's," Jake said as he was putting on his coat.

Trader Vic's was a famous Tiki Bar in the basement of the Plaza Hotel where they offered good but inauthentic Asian food. They had a whole section on the menu called Cantonese Supper which had Fuji Beef as an option. Wrong country, but it didn't matter. People flocked there anyway because the atmosphere was fun and the drinks were generous.

Cara, Ginny and Jake took the bus down to the Thalia theater. Being Saturday, it was packed, but they managed to get three seats together in the small dark auditorium.

The movie began with a young man trying to fake his own suicide for fun. Not for fun actually, but to get his parent's attention. Then the young man meets an eccentric much older woman who "gets him" and they fall in love. Cara and Ginny sat in the dark loving it. What a crazy, fun wacky film they thought. Ginny sat next to Jake in the theater and felt him glancing at her several times, just making sure she was enjoying the film.

Afterwards, he walked the girls across Broadway to the uptown bus stop and gave Cara and Ginny money for the bus.

"Since I'm close to home I'm gonna head there from here. Have a fun dinner tonight," Jake said, and kissed them both on the cheek. They boarded the bus uptown.

Jake was thinking how big his niece Cara had gotten and Ginny too. He couldn't help seeing that Ginny was becoming beautiful, with her large brown eyes and shapely figure.

That following Monday, when Cara arrived home, Connie was already waiting in the hallway by the front door. She was holding an envelope.

"Oh my God, is that from Music and Art?" Cara said, eyes wide.

Connie nodded, "I didn't open it, you should," Cara grabbed the envelope and tore it open. She read the letter.

"I'm in!" Cara yelled out jumping up and down.

"I should call Ginny so we can celebrate together."

"Let her be for a bit Cara. She just got home too, I'm sure, and she will want to tell her family. Give her an hour," Connie said.

Cara waited watching the clock. She couldn't wait to leave St. Hilda's and go to the coolest school in the city with her best friend in the world.

Finally, after an hour, she dialed Ginny's number. Ginny's older sister Sara answered and she excitedly asked for Ginny.

Sara said, "Cara, Ginny is in her room. She's upset and says she wants to be left alone. Cara, Ginny wasn't accepted to Music and Art."

Chapter Nine

Jake felt irritated when Amanda called the morning after their trip to say, "They needed to talk." He felt put upon. Why should he have to stay at home just because she might call to say good night? His friend Mark called the night they returned to welcome him home and asked him to grab a beer. So they went to a local bar. He knew he wasn't ready to play house with Amanda, even though they spoke about it, and he agreed. Amanda continued, that she was looking for more in a relationship, that she didn't want to compete with his friends and that she felt they both needed to move on. He wanted to protest, to tell her he was sorry, and that he loved her, but instead he found himself saying "If that's what you really want, don't let me stop you. I want you to be happy." Amanda then started crying and hung up. He tried to call her back, but she didn't pick up. Jesus, he thought, I don't need this.

Two weeks later Jake invited Luke and Mark for a weekend at his family country house at Lake George. The weather was brisk for April, but sunny and it would be good to get away. They all agreed.

It was a long drive to Lake George, so they stopped for dinner in Albany, and then continued north to the small roads leading to Glen Lake Road. Jake loved that old house that his grandfather had built. It was a log cabin style home with four bedrooms and three baths. There had been many upgrades since his grandfather built it, each making it more modern and comfortable. The kitchen was expansive, and outside the back door was a large porch where one could look down the lawn leading to the small dock on the lake. A small wooden row boat was tied there.

Being at the house brought back happy memories of childhood summers. Jake's father, who also spent summers there as a child, would take Jake and Connie in the rowboat and they would fish, and if they caught anything, their mother cooked the fish for dinner that night. Summer evenings were a lot of fun with Connie teaching Jake card games, or the whole family playing charades.

He missed his father and mother. They both passed away many years ago. His father died from throat cancer when Jake was twenty-three and his mother two years later from a heart attack. There was some money left to him and Connie, which helped even though Connie was working already. Today, he and Connie pooled their resources to pay the taxes and any upkeep. There were no memories of the house in winters because it was not winterized. Heavy blankets were in every room.

April was not the best month to visit, but Jake, Mark and Luke had a great time going to Topps for drinks, and dinner at Vincent's. During the day they hiked, and spoke about fishing in the summer. They also talked about girlfriends. At that time, Luke was the only one in a relationship. Jake and Amanda hadn't spoken in two weeks, and as far as he was concerned, they were finished. Jake was a great date, he confessed, but a difficult boyfriend.

Jake felt good to be with his buddies again. Mark was like him, easy going and single. Luke on the other hand was jumping into his relationship with Anna so quickly that Jake thought of telling him to take it slowly, but he didn't. Friends had a way of drifting away when he expressed advice about their relationships. Jake shared that he developed a feeling of claustrophobia once a relationship had settled in. There were expectations that gnawed at him. Sure, he wanted to love someone, but it had to be on his terms, with his timing. He loved the courtship. That was exciting. But when it was clear he had gotten the woman, he became bored and needed a new challenge.

Chapter Ten

The bell rang at noon and the students in Cara's live drawing class picked up their backpacks, walked into the large hallway, down the stairs and into the sunshine to eat their bagged lunches, or grab something from the many food trucks. Cara never brought a bagged lunch from home. Instead, she either bought a knish or empanadas. On cold or rainy days Cara and her friends would go to the City College cafeteria. City College never checked IDs. The more conservative kids ate in the Music and Art cafeteria, but Cara and her friends were Hippy wannabes. They thought they were so cool hanging out with the college kids.

Cara loved going to school there. Her first friend was Lina in her sculpting class. Lina loved to work on animal figures and busts. She was a full-figured blond, and wore round red sunglasses that she never took off, even indoors.

Then there were Jason and Matt.

Jason, born in Puerto Rico, came here as a baby. He had long wavy hair, wore carpenter pants and walked with a nonchalant swagger. He was also one of the best illustrators at school. His work was displayed at Lever House, as well as in small shops in Greenwich Village who sold them on consignment. Matt was tall and blond, and dressed conservatively, although he always looked as though he needed a haircut. He was a piano virtuoso, and had already performed in Town Hall and other notable venues around the city.

Cara's classes were filled with energy and amazing talent. The teachers challenged the students in many ways, such as giving them projects to design using found objects or incorporating painting and drawing on the same canvas. Cara would hear the music students practicing in the hallways and admired them so much because she couldn't play any instrument at all. Then there were the Vocal Music majors who sang their hearts out in the school and outside. Sometimes there would be impromptu performances at lunchtime.

It was October 1975, and since both her parents worked, Cara invited her friends home from Music and Art. After they arrived, she dialed Ginny's number.

"We're all here, come on down!" Cara told Ginny.

Two minutes later Ginny walked in, all smiles, ready to hangout. Matt produced a joint. They sat in Cara's living room with all the windows open. Each took tokes as they passed the joint around. Curls of smoke filled the room, along with their laughter. Cara glanced at Ginny who was looking at Matt, smiling. Matt looked like Peter Tork from The Monkees. Ginny had a crush on Matt and felt shy around him. She was unaware that she had grown up to be quite a beauty. The only person Ginny was not shy around was Cara.

Jason and Lina were already a couple, and sat together on a bean bag chair. Lina had already confessed to Cara that they had gone "all the way". Cara couldn't understand what the fuss was about. She herself wanted to wait. They were all seventeen and eighteen years old and in their senior year. No one knew yet where they would attend college in the fall.

Ginny did not follow her passion for music after her rejection from Music and Art. Instead, she applied to colleges where she could pursue liberal arts. Ginny actually wanted to take a year off and travel, or just take time to work and save money, but her mother wouldn't hear of it. She applied to NYU, Barnard in New York and Bennington College in Vermont.

They all hung out until five o' clock when Cara said her parents would be home soon. Matt, Lina and Jason left. Ginny stayed., and the two went around with magazines fanning the air toward the open windows to get rid of the pot scent. The wind outside just blew the smoke back inside. They both laughed at that.

Then Cara stopped to look at her reflection in the hallway mirror. "I hate the way I look. I'm too skinny, flat chested and have this curly red hair I can't control."

"Don't be ridiculous, you're beautiful," Ginny said. But Cara realized they were no longer two little girls. They were young women moving forward in their lives. She looked at Ginny, her friend of fifteen years. and saw that Ginny's shyness as a child, was now part of her charm. Her awkwardness had turned into a kind and gentle persona.

Cara always felt good around Ginny.

Chapter Eleven

Graduation Day was a beautiful spring day in May 1976. Under her black graduation gown, Cara wore her favorite blue print dress with spaghetti straps and new Kork-Ease sandals. The graduation was at Carnegie Hall, which Mel and Connie thought was amazing. Billy Dee Williams and Erica Jong delivered the commencement speeches. Both had graduated from Music and Art in the 50s.

Cara, Mel, Connie, Jake and his new girlfriend Rose went to the Russian Tea Room for a celebration lunch. They sat at a large booth and looked at the huge menus that hid their faces. In April she had learned she was accepted into both the School of Visual Arts and RISD. She wanted to stay in New York City, so she decided on Visual Arts. She would live at home the first year, and save her parents money.

At the Russian Tea Room, Cara ordered the Boeuf à la Stroganoff and looked around the red dining room with its overstuffed booths in red leather, deep green walls and lacquered wooden ceiling. She looked at her father whom she adored and saw that he looked tired. He had been having trouble sleeping. She overheard Connie telling Mel to quit drinking so much and that would help. She didn't say it kindly. She sounded harsh, and Cara felt sorry for her father. He never raised his voice to her mother, nor anyone else for that matter. Connie sat with a stern look on her face trying to get the waiter's attention for more water.

Cara looked at Jake and then Jake's girlfriend Rose wondering how long this one would last. She could tell by the angle of Jake's arm that he was resting his hand somewhere on Rose's thigh under the table. Rose was all dolled up in a tight-fitting yellow dress that was cut way too low. She was dressed for a date that would end up in the bedroom, not for a family lunch. Her blond hair was piled high up on her head and her makeup looked as though she stopped at Bloomingdale's that morning for a "Makeover Special." Jake reached into his jacket and pulled out a gift-wrapped box and handed it over the table to Cara. She unwrapped it to find a beautiful gold bracelet. She thanked Jake and put it on immediately, beaming. Everyone smiled at Cara except for Rose who gave a smirk. Cara ordered the Chocolate Mousse Cake for dessert and they all raised their glasses to say "congratulations."

Chapter Twelve

It was the October 1978 and Jake was going downtown to Greenwich Village to have lunch with Ross Banner, the creative director of Benton & Bowles, to discuss a new client. Jake and Ross met at Minetta Tavern. B & B was expanding and changing. General Petroleum Oil (Mobil Oil) needed a new approach. They discussed the launch of the Energy for a Strong America campaign over Soup à l'Onion and Coq au Vin. The lunch included drinks too, with gin and tonics and vodka martinis. It was understood that the day ended after lunch.

Jake left the Minetta Tavern at three in the afternoon with a buzz. At forty-five degrees, it was nippy, almost wintry. He walked uptown along sixth avenue and past boutiques, pizza parlors and smoke shops. He noticed the abundance of homeless people. He thought of his sister Connie and the homeless problem around Columbia University that had gotten so bad. He knew the University would do something about it. The parents of those students attending the college surely would demand something be done. Of course, his old neighborhood at 98th and Broadway was no better. He often had to step over someone to get into a store.

Jake had moved to the Upper East Side a year ago and never wanted to look back.

Jake stopped at a small Italian deli near 8th Street to pick up the spicy salami he loved to keep around his apartment. A little bell rang as he opened the door. He stood behind a woman who was paying for her order. When she turned around, he saw her.

"Well, well, Ginny, hi! What are you doing in this neighborhood?" he asked.

"Jake, wonderful to see you! I'm attending NYU and live around the corner," Ginny said, as she gave him a hug.

"Oh of course, Cara did mention that to me. Gosh I haven't seen you in a while. I think the last time was your high school graduation more than two years ago. You look great!" Jake said.

What he really wanted to say was "God you've grown up to be such a gorgeous woman."

The little bell above the entrance door rang again. Jake moved aside to let an elderly woman place her order.

"Well, it was great running into you," Ginny said. "Don't let me keep you from ordering. Hope to see you again soon."

"Wait, listen I come down here quite a bit for work," Jake lied, then continued. "Let me take you to dinner sometime. I'll see when I'm going to be down here and we can plan something."

"That would be great, sure," Ginny said.

"Give me your number. It will be fun to go somewhere charming down here for a meal, no?"

Jake worried that he implied that she must only eat cafeteria food so here he was to the rescue.

Ginny smiled and reached into her purse for a pen. The customer finished her order and moved past them to exit. Ginny asked the man behind the counter for scrap paper. He tore off a piece of sandwich wrapping paper. She jotted down her phone number and handed it to Jake. He gave her a kiss on the cheek and a hug before Ginny turned to leave.

Jake continued his stroll uptown after leaving the deli thinking of Ginny. He thought to himself how nice it would be to have dinner with her. It would be a kind uncle-like thing to do for a young student on her own at college. He thought of The Coach House just off Waverly Place. It was in a nineteenth century building that was once the estate of the Wanamaker family. Yes, he said to himself, he would take her there. As he continued to walk, he thought that maybe he should invite Cara as well. Wouldn't Ginny mention the dinner to Cara? Wouldn't it be weird for him to have dinner with Ginny without Cara? This is ridiculous, he concluded. He would just take Ginny to dinner as a gesture to an old friend of his niece and he should stop over-thinking it.

Chapter Thirteen

Ginny thought it was funny running into Jake in her neighborhood. He was upbeat and lighthearted, so she looked forward to having dinner with him. But she also felt awkward. Would he tell Cara? Would he invite Cara? She shrugged it off and told herself it was a friendly dinner with an old friend. Cara and Ginny had stayed close during the start of college. Last summer Ginny even spent two weeks with Cara and her family at Lake George. They were both immersed in school lately and she hadn't spoken to Cara in weeks. She made a mental note to call and see her the following week.

Ginny had met boys at NYU these past two years and had gone on a couple dates to a bowling alley and the local pizza place, but the dates never went anywhere. She was completely inexperienced and so were the boys. She told herself she would probably meet someone after she graduated, when she was working.

Ginny walked to her apartment that she shared with her roommate, Jane. The apartment felt cold. She went to the small living room and turned on a space heater. Jane must have been at class. She didn't love the apartment, but it was cheap and temporary. Also, she didn't have much of a choice. Her mother, Barbara, had announced that after Ginny graduated from high school, she would move to California. Her older sister Sara had left the apartment three years before to live with her boyfriend, Adrian. Ginny lived in the dorm her freshman year, but when Jane, who was in her writing class, invited her to be her roommate, she jumped at the chance.

Ginny sat on the couch next to the warmth of the heater. She reached for her notebook and pen that were on the coffee table and started to write. Her assignment for her Contemporary Writing course was to pick a subject that meant something to her and which also affects the general population. The title of her essay was *Poverty and Homelessness in the United States*. She wrote that when people see a homeless person or someone suffering in poverty, people assumed that the homeless person must have done something wrong to cause their situation. Sometimes people blamed mental illness. Some people live paycheck to paycheck with no safety net. One bad thing happens to them, and wham they are in trouble. Ginny cited examples of how society treated these people, and how that just fueled the problem. Ginny loved to write. She loved to disappear into her writing with her thoughts and feelings.

That evening, Ginny reached for the phone.

"Hi Cara, it's me."

"Hey stranger! How are you?" Cara said.

"I'm good. I've been bogged down with schoolwork and feel like I have no life," Ginny said, chuckling.

"Ughh I know the feeling. Hey, what are you up to Saturday? Want to come to the old neighborhood? My dad is home sick with a bad cough, but we can step out somewhere."

"Yes, great. I'd love to see Mel and Connie. I haven't seen them since the summer."

They hung up and Ginny realized that she hadn't mentioned running into Jake. She thought she'd see how the conversation went when she saw Cara and decide then how to bring it up.

The following evening, she was in the kitchen making herself a snack of cheese and crackers when the phone rang. Jane was near the phone in the living room and picked it up.

"Sure, hold on. Ginny, it's for you," Jane said.

"Who?" Ginny mouthed with no sound. Jane shrugged and silently mouthed back, "a man."

It was Jake. He sounded charming and told Ginny he was going to be in her neighborhood next Wednesday and that he chose a great place to take her to dinner. He asked for her address and said he would pick her up at seven. She said "perfect" and looked forward to it. There was no mention of Cara.

That Saturday, Ginny headed to her old apartment building in the late afternoon. It felt strange coming here again. It had only been a couple of years but seemed like a lifetime ago. She pressed the buzzer of apt 5A. Connie opened the door and gave her a big hug, smiling. Cara hugged her too and they all sat in the living room catching up. Ginny asked about Mel just as she heard movement to the left of the living room. Mel was in a bathrobe and shuffled in to just say hello. Mel looked so pale and thin. He coughed and then headed back to his bedroom.

Ginny looked at Connie and asked "Has Mel seen a doctor for his cough? It seems bad."

"Mel has been stubborn as usual, but I'm forcing him to go this coming week. It's lasted awhile and it's affecting his teaching."

Cara looked down and seemed upset. "Mom please go with him on that visit so you can hear what the doctor says. Dad can just gloss things over some times."

"I will Cara, now you guys go on and have a good night," Connie said.

Cara and Ginny went one block down Broadway to the West End Bar. They sat at a quiet booth in the back that had deep carved names and initials in the dark wooden table. Cara told Ginny that she had decided to become a book illustrator, maybe working on book covers or children's books. She loved imagining the images that went with the story. She told her how she did an illustration for *Fahrenheit 451* that won the highest grade in the class.

Ginny then asked about Mel. Cara said he had been sick off and on for several weeks. It was terrible because her parents had been fighting too. Her mother was scared, but she showed it with anger.

Then Cara said, "I'm scared too."

Ginny reached over to take Cara's hands in hers. She held them for a while and it seemed Cara didn't want to release them.

"Cara, you know I'm always here for you," Ginny said.

"I know. I love you," Cara said.

Ginny smiled and said, "Love you too."

When they parted Ginny realized there had been no appropriate time to mention Jake.

Chapter Fourteen

It was windy and cold that morning as Cara headed toward the School of Visual Arts when she heard her name being called. It was Jason, catching up with her as she headed to the school entrance. They had the same Creative Ads course that taught attention grabbing skills for commercials, billboards and subway posters.

Cara and Jason shared several classes even though he was leaning toward advertising and she toward illustration. Jason had the same macho swagger, but had now dropped the carpenter pants for khakis and denim. He was planning to get his own place soon. Although he stayed in touch with Lina, he didn't see her often after they broke up. When class ended, Jason said he wanted to try the new Chinese restaurant on 18th Street called Plum Garden. They agreed to go the following night.

Cara kept re-thinking the other evening with Ginny. She had dominated their conversation about her art classes and her father and didn't give Ginny a chance to say a word about herself. Cara thought she would call Ginny soon, and this time she would just listen.

The next evening Cara saw Jason waiting in front of Plum Garden, smiling as she walked up. Jason's confident air was augmented by his handsome Hispanic features, freshly pressed striped shirt and khakis. Cara wore just what she had worn to school that day and hadn't bothered to change so she felt a little frumpy next to him.

"Look at you, all handsome and sharp!" Cara said.

Jason smiled and held the restaurant door open. Plum Garden was filled with lanterns and paper dragons in slithering positions on the ceiling. They were shown to a corner table for two. They were both hungry so when the fast-speaking waiter arrived, they ordered Kung Pao chicken and the Crispy Fish with Special Sauce. They talked about their classes and what courses they wanted to take next semester. Jason had always been so reassuring and comforting.

When the bill came, she reached into her purse.

"No, this is on me," Jason said. She at least wanted to split the bill, but he insisted. When they left the restaurant, Cara was going to take the subway uptown.

"I'll walk with you," Jason said even though he lived within walking distance in the opposite direction.

They chatted until they reached the subway entrance. Then when they went to hug goodbye Jason turned his face toward hers and leaned in to kiss her. Cara was taken by surprise and pulled back a bit, but then leaned into him for the kiss. They kissed and then hugged each other.

"I've always had feelings for you Cara," Jason said, as he took her hand looking at her.

Cara didn't know what to say so she just hugged him again. Jason said he'd call her and asked if they could see each other that weekend. She nodded and headed into the subway. Cara wasn't sure what to feel as she rode the subway uptown. She was surprised and confused. She liked Jason very much. He was a good friend. Did she want to change that? This was her first real kiss. Spin The Bottle at one of Lina's high school parties didn't count. She hadn't even dated anyone in high school or college so far. Truthfully it never bothered her because she had not been attracted to anyone. Was she attracted to Jason? She decided to see where this goes. She can't become one of those odd people who never have any partners their whole life. Besides, she liked Jason, there was history with him, and, she had to admit, he was good looking.

The subway stopped at the 116th Street station, Cara got off and headed the one block south to her apartment building.

When she entered her apartment, her mother was sitting quietly at the kitchen table looking down.

"Mom, what's wrong?" she asked.

"The X-rays came back. Mel has stage 4 lung cancer."

Chapter Fifteen

Since his promotion to overseeing the entire Proctor and Gamble account, Jake was busy. He was happy, but felt he deserved it. He had been working very hard, and thought dinner with Ginny at The Coach House would be a great way to celebrate.

Jake called Iris, the woman he had been seeing for over a year now, to cancel her visit for that Wednesday, telling her he had to work late. Iris seemed disappointed, but said she understood. He liked Iris. She was a petite woman who wore her jet-black hair in a pixie cut. She was into eating right, growing her own vegetables in the summer at her parent's home on Long Island and practicing yoga. She had herbs that she grew on the kitchen shelf by her window, and she sometimes brought herbs to his apartment when she cooked dinner for him. Jake thought she might be a good influence. She usually went to his place because she had a tiny studio in the east 80s. They met at a party that Luke and Anna had thrown. They started dating and always had a great time together. The sex was also very good.

"Iris and I have great sexual chemistry. She is game for anything. What I also like is her easy-going attitude. No fuss, no clinging, no questions, it's just easy," Jake told his friend Mark.

Mark was seeing Felicia, a woman he had met at work about a year ago, and sometimes they double dated with Jake and Iris. Mark called that Monday to ask about double dating to see the movie, *The Boys from Brazil* that was opening Wednesday.

"Unfortunately, I can't man, I've got a date. Let's plan for Saturday," Jake said.

"Are you taking Iris somewhere new and fun?". Mark asked.

"No, listen it's not with Iris, so please don't say anything when we all get together," Jake said.

Mark hated when Jake asked him to lie because even if it never came up, he knew the lie was in his heart.

"So, I'll see you Saturday," Jake said. "We can all catch the movie then. I'll look up the movie times and call you tomorrow."

"Jake, I can't make it Saturday. Felicia and I already have plans," Mark lied this time to Jake.

Wednesday came and Jake stopped home to freshen up before picking up Ginny for dinner. He was looking forward to it, and to asking her about her courses, her plans, her future. He decided to wear a dark gray suit and the expensive cologne he saved for special occasions.

Jake grabbed a taxi downtown to Ginny's address on 9th Street. The apartment building was filled with young students. The intercom crackled as Ginny's voice asked who it was. He answered and she told him she'd be right down. He observed the students coming and going in and out of the lobby. God, he could be their father, he thought. This will just be a simple evening out taking a young lady to have a sophisticated dinner with an older family friend who will introduce her to another side of life, Jake told himself. She can then know what she should expect and want from dating because the bar has been raised by him.

Ginny exited the building looking radiant in a fitted black coat, heels and her hair pulled into a bun. Jake looked at her admiringly.

"You look beautiful Ginny!" Jake blurted out.

"Oh, thank you," Ginny said, shyly.

They spoke about her day and her classes as they walked to The Coach House. When they arrived, Jake held the door open. As they entered the brick and wood paneled restaurant. he checked their coats. Ginny was wearing a long-sleeved black sweater and black and red plaid skirt. She looked around and felt awkward. Maybe she should have worn her burgundy dress. She was not used to going out to dinner in such places. The maitre'd then brought them to a red leather banquette.

"Jake, this place is beautiful," Ginny said as she looked around at the 19th century oil paintings on the walls of the gently lit room.

"You must try the crab cakes and the roast duck here. Also, the steak au poivre is amazing!"

Ginny just nodded, feeling very insecure. Jake kept the conversation going by asking Ginny about her classes and what she saw herself doing in the future. He made her feel more at ease as the evening went on.

"I want to be a writer, although I'm not sure what kind of writing I want to do. Maybe I'll try journalism, I'm not sure," Ginny told him.

Jake was encouraging and told her that she should pursue her passion. If she ever wanted to show her work to him, he would love to read it. Before they ordered dinner, Jake called the waiter over and ordered a bottle of champagne.

"I want to celebrate with you. I just got a promotion at work. It's been a busy year, but it's paid off," Jake said, smiling at Ginny.

"Wow, congratulations Jake!"

They spoke more about his job and the accounts he had. He told her about the CLIO awards in advertising coming up and how much fun it was to watch the commercials of the nominees. He invited her to come to a screening one day soon. The champagne arrived and the waiter filled her flute. Jake continued to ask Ginny more about her goals and her family and the waiter kept pouring the champagne. Dinner arrived. Ginny ordered the steak and Jake had the roast duck. Jake went ahead and ordered a bottle of red wine to go with their meals.

When dinner was finished Jake insisted that she have the chocolate cake. Ginny agreed, feeling woozy. One glass of wine at a special occasion was the most she ever drank. This night, she was consuming a lot more than she was used to. When dinner was over and she stood up, she felt unstable in her heels. Jake smiled and came around to her chair to take her arm as they got their coats to leave. Ginny managed to sober up a bit as they walked back to her apartment. She stopped just to the right of the front door.

"Jake, thank you. I had a great time and what a wonderful restaurant that was. Congratulations on your promotion," Ginny said, hoping her words were not slurred.

"I had a great time, Ginny. I'll see when the screenings are for the CLIO award nominees and I'll let you know."

Jake leaned in and gave Ginny a hug. As he held her, he moved his hand down her back and pulled her toward him to kiss her and then decided to turn his head to kiss her cheek. As he held her, he could feel his body react. He could smell her hair and feel her body under her coat. God, what was he doing, he thought. Jake watched her as she entered the building and then hailed a taxi to take him uptown.

He had fun. Everything was new for Ginny and she had her whole life ahead of her. Jake looked at his watch, it was only ten thirty. It was early, but Ginny had classes tomorrow, so he hadn't wanted to ask her for a nightcap.

Jake entered his apartment, turned on the soft light by the entryway. He then moved to the wall phone and dialed a number.

Iris answered.

Chapter Sixteen

"How was your night out?" Jane asked.

"Pretty great," Ginny answered as she leaned against the wall near her front door to steady herself.

"A little too much to drink?" Jane asked, chuckling.

"How old is this guy?" Jane continued.

"Mid-forties, but he's young for his age. God Jane, the restaurant was so beautiful and the food was fantastic," Ginny said.

"The drinks too I see. How do you know him?" Jane asked.

Ginny walked slowly to the couch and sat down without taking her coat off.

"I've known him all my life really. He's the uncle of Cara. You've met Cara."

"Oh yes, the skinny redhead that's come over," Jane said.

"She's my oldest and dearest friend. Her uncle was downtown and just wanted to take me out to celebrate his promotion," Ginny said, as she started to remove her coat.

"Really, just you? I don't know, it sounds like a date to me," Jane said as she stood up and headed to her bedroom.

After listening to Jane, Ginny started to question why Cara never came up in their conversation at dinner. Why was he celebrating his advancement at work with just her?

She decided to let it go.

The following day Ginny woke up with a headache and decided to skip her class that morning. She wasn't sure what to make of last night. She was enjoying herself at dinner, and then when Jake brought her to her building, she knew that he had wanted to kiss her, but decided otherwise. Ginny was confused. She felt drawn to Jake, but the feeling seemed inappropriate. Jake was always fun to be with. Now she saw how charming and seductive he could be as well.

Ginny made her afternoon class. It was already full, but she found her seat. The teaching assistant was passing around graded papers from the previous week. She received an A on her Poverty essay from her Contemporary Writing professor. Her next assignment was to write about an uncomfortable situation that happened to you or someone you know. Ginny laughed to herself.

On her way home she thought she should call Cara. Maybe Jake mentioned the dinner to her? When she walked into her apartment, Jane was home. They spoke for a bit, then Ginny took the kitchen phone into her bedroom and dialed Cara's number. Cara answered and told Ginny about Mel's diagnosis and that he was starting Chemotherapy the following week.

"My God Cara, let me come to you, or do you want to come here?" Ginny asked.

"Actually, I'd love to come by you if you're free now. I need to see you," Cara said.

Ginny told her to come immediately and she should stay for dinner. Ginny felt distraught. Mel was such a good man. This should never have happened to him.

Just as she hung up the phone rang. it was Jake.

"Ginny, I just wanted to tell you what a great time I had with you last night. I..." Jake was interrupted by Ginny asking him if he had spoken to Cara or Connie lately.

"I've been so busy that I've been remiss. Connie left me a message at work yesterday, but I haven't had a chance to call her back." Jake said quickly, nervous about what it could be.

"Jake, Mel has cancer and it doesn't sound good. I feel awful for Cara. She's coming over soon." Ginny said.

"Oh my God, thank you for telling me, I'll call Connie now," Jake said and paused.

"Ginny, I won't tell Connie that you told me the news. I'm sure that's why she called me and I'll let her tell me herself."

"That's fine. I won't mention to Cara that we spoke either." Ginny said, paused, then added "I had a great time last night too." She hung up feeling sick about hiding something from Cara, but understood the complications if Jake had heard the news from her.

A half hour later Cara buzzed to come up. Jane left to have dinner with a friend thinking Ginny would want time with Cara alone.

Ginny opened the door and gave Cara a huge hug. Cara burst into tears.

They ordered pizza and sat in the living room, talking. Cara felt so helpless, and now Connie was angry all the time.

"I know my mother needs me, but she tries to act as though she doesn't need anyone. She's always been that way, pushing people away as though she's ready to face the battle alone. When I reach out to her, she just says she's fine," Cara told Ginny.

Cara was sitting next to Ginny and as she spoke Ginny moved closer and took her hand. As before Cara held her hand for a while.

Cara then said, "Remember I've mentioned Jason? We're in some of the same classes. We've spent a lot of time going to movies and grabbing dinner. I've always liked him, and he's been a great friend. Our friendship took a turn recently. After dinner he walked me to the subway. When we said good night, he kissed me."

"Really? You've known each other for so long."

"It's sort of weird, I always thought fireworks are supposed to go off when someone kisses you. Honestly, I didn't feel anything. My heart didn't skip a beat, there were no butterflies in my stomach, nothing. But then I think, what could I know about how I should feel? I've never been with anyone."

"Maybe he could be a comfort to you during this time," Ginny told her.

Cara looked at Ginny and asked "Would you mind if I stayed over? I just feel like I need to be away tonight. I think everything is getting to me."

"Of course! I'll give you a nightgown and it will be like old times with our sleepovers," Ginny said reassuringly.

Cara went to the phone and called her mother to ask about Mel and to let her know she would see her in the morning. She then went to Ginny's bedroom.

Cara and Ginny changed into their nightgowns and sat on Ginny's bed talking about the fun times they used to have as children. Cara was happy to be able to take her mind off her father's illness. Cara looked at Ginny feeling so lucky to have her in her life.

As she lay next to Ginny in the queen bed that night, she felt her heart skip a beat.

Chapter Seventeen

Iris sat up in bed in Jake's new apartment on East 86th Street. She leaned over to kiss him still lying beside her. She was beautiful, with olive skin, small delicate features, and green eyes that stood out from the hood of her short black hair. Her body was slim and fit from her yoga and the cycling she had started doing. Three loops around Central Park every other morning.

Iris dressed, smiled at Jake and said, "I'm heading out. Call me later and tell me how things are after you see your sister and her husband. Hope I get a chance to meet them one day."

"I will, thank you," Jake said, ignoring the meeting his family statement.

Iris visited either Friday or Saturday night, and sometimes during the week if they both felt the urge. They would have amazing sex, she would sleep over, and in the morning, they would go at it again. She told him about cardio workouts he should try, and advised him about nutrition. His cholesterol and blood pressure were high, so he really should listen to her, he thought. On those afternoons after she stayed over, they had breakfast or lunch, then she'd go home to her place. Jake set the tone early in their relationship that she stayed only one night, and Iris was fine with that.

Jake called Connie after speaking to Ginny, and she told him about Mel. He went right away that night to see Connie and Cara. They spoke about the treatment Mel would receive and for how long. Jake saw the panic in Connie's eyes. Cara was there and he caught up with her. Connie was preparing a chicken dinner and invited him to stay. During dinner Connie asked if he was seeing anyone.

"No, dating here and there, but nobody special," Jake said.

He had gotten tired of Connie teasing about his "serial dating" and never settling down with one woman, so he stopped telling her about his dates. Some of his old friends were now married and had pulled away, moving onto their "settled" lives with wives, kids, mortgages and other responsibilities. Jake found it easier to find new single male friends, some never married and some divorced, with whom he could hang around. He met his new friends at bars or when he vacationed at Club Med. He vacationed at Club Med every year for New Year's Eve week, so he would not have to pop champagne with anyone who would expect something serious. He met women at Club Med who just wanted to have fun, and for those seven days it was a blast. Then he would come home and resume his responsibility free lifestyle. Sometimes he would meet a like-minded friend that he would continue to hang out with until that friend got hooked by a woman who wanted more.

Jake thought of Ginny. She was innocent and unspoiled by what life eventually brings. It was obvious that he was showing Ginny a new world by taking her to The Coach House and it was fun to introduce her to things and see that wide eyed look on her face. It had been two weeks since he saw her. He reached for the phone and dialed her number. She wasn't home, but he left a message with her roommate Jane. After watching some TV and having a cognac he thought he'd try her again, but then thought that he was pursuing too much.

At ten thirty his phone rang. It was Ginny saying she was sorry she missed his call.

"Ginny, I wanted to let you know that I just saw Connie and Mel. I think things will be okay. Mel's going for treatment and there have been so many advancements over the years, so Mel will get the proper care," Jake said.

"Oh, that's great to hear. I hope he'll be okay," Ginny said.

"I also called to let you know they have started screenings of the CLIO nominations. They are Wednesdays and Fridays. Are you free on one of those days this coming week?"

"That sounds like fun. I could use a break from studying. Wednesday is bad because I have a test on Thursday, so let's do Friday."

"Wonderful. Would you mind coming to my office at five o'clock and we'll go to the screening room in the building. After that, I'll take you to dinner."

That week was very busy for Jake. B & B was expanding globally and opening offices in Australia, Hong Kong, Germany, Spain. Kenya and South Africa. There was a discussion that Jake would travel to Hong Kong next month to help facilitate the Proctor and Gamble presence there.

He remembered to call Iris on Thursday to tell her that this weekend he would see her Saturday.

At five on Friday Ginny rode the elevator to the 2nd floor to the offices at Benton & Bowles. She asked for Jake Baines at the reception. This time she wore her burgundy dress. Ginny wondered if she had overdressed for the evening. The dress fit her figure perfectly. Her chestnut hair was worn down around her shoulders and she looked beautiful. Jake couldn't hide his admiring look on his face when he saw her.

He noticed some of his co-workers turning their heads as she passed with him to the screening room. He was proud to be with her.

They watched the automobile, cereal, toothpaste, bath tissue, shaving cream and insurance commercials from all over the world that were nominated for CLIO awards in different categories. Most were either very funny or touching in the way they conveyed their products or services. It lasted only an hour, which was plenty for showing one- and two-minute commercials. Jake was sitting next to Ginny occasionally glancing over at her. She was having a great time.

When the screenings were finished Jake and Ginny left the building and jumped into a taxi to go to the Top of The Sixes at 666 Fifth Avenue. As they rode the elevator up to the restaurant, Ginny told Jake which commercials she liked. She told him she enjoyed the foreign ones the best; that they had a different feel and approach to selling a product. Jake told her what it took to make a commercial and how difficult some of the actors could be.

They had a table by the window and the city lights were shining below them. Ginny looked around at the beautiful people in this elegant restaurant and felt as though she were floating on air. She looked at Jake and saw how handsome he was. When he looked at her, she felt herself being pulled toward him. Ginny spoke about her latest school assignments, but preferred to listen to details about his job.

As dessert was being finished, Jake asked "You know I've moved to 86th Street just off Madison Avenue. Would you like to see it? I have cognac, brandy, sambuca, or just plain ginger ale. I'm decorating the apartment now and could use a woman's touch, so maybe you could tell me what I need. We'll just stay awhile and then I'll call a car service to take you home."

"Sure, for just a bit." Ginny said feeling awkward about going to his place. She told herself she would stay a half hour, advise Jake on his decor, even though she didn't know much about that, and then take a car home.

They grabbed another taxi to his apartment, where the doorman greeted them at the curb. They rode up to the tenth floor. Jake's apartment was a one bedroom with a den that could have been a second bedroom. He still had his black leather couch from his old apartment, but now he had added more modern furniture and furnishings. He had a bar cart in the living room and large slipper chairs in front of his couch.

Ginny came in shyly and admired the apartment. Jake asked her about the lighting and if he should have a lamp here or there as he walked over to the bar and took out two small glasses.

"Would you like some sambuca?" Jake asked.

Ginny said she didn't know what it was, but that she would try it. He walked into the kitchen and took out four coffee beans to place a couple in each glass. On the leather couch Ginny sipped her sambuca. She felt tipsy and began to talk about the Bond film *Moonraker* that had just opened and that she heard was very good. She started to feel nervous, and rambled on about his lighting, and where lamps should go. Jake went to the stereo and put on a Jobim album. He sat next to her on the leather couch. He slowly sipped his drink and listened to her. He didn't say anything, he just watched and listened. He could sense her nervousness. After some time, Jake looked at her and put one hand on her shoulder and the other around her waist and slowly pulled her toward him. Then he moved one hand to the side of her face and gently kissed her on her mouth. Ginny felt her body collapse into his arms. It was as if she couldn't control herself. There was no reasoning, no thought, just the pull of her body to him. He started kissing her neck, then the top of her shoulder and then one hand was on her breast over her dress. Jake then stood up, took her hands to help her stand next to him and led her to the bedroom.

"I've never..." Ginny started to say.

"Shhh, don't worry, let me take care of everything."

Chapter Eighteen

Ginny was writing in her composition notebook having trouble concentrating. She felt happy and excited, but also anxious. Ginny had been seeing Jake for about four weeks. Never before had she felt so physically drawn to someone. Jake had awoken her sexuality, and made her aware of its power. When she was with him, she let him guide and teach her, looking to him for knowledge and expertise in whatever they were doing. He had taken her to an exhibit at MoMA, and to a jazz concert at the Blue Note. She was having a wonderful time and taking everything in.

Jake also took her shopping and bought her more dresses. He bought her expensive jewelry, too, to replace the cheap silver she had bought in the Village. Initially she felt very uncomfortable accepting such gifts, but Jake insisted and that became part of pleasing him.

Ginny saw Jake on Friday, and sometimes on a weekday night. Over the weekend he told her he had projects to work on, and must prepare for his Monday morning meetings. She completely understood. She also understood when he told her he needed "downtime", and vacationed without her New Year's week. Cara was never mentioned when they were together, and Ginny waited for his lead to address that relationship.

That Saturday, Ginny was meeting Cara to go to a Red Grooms exhibit at a gallery in the East 50s.

Ginny put her notebook down and looked at her watch. She saw she was running late and rushed to get dressed. She ran to the subway uptown and was ten minutes late to meet Cara who was waiting at the front door. They hugged and went in.

Red Grooms was the perfect artist for both of them to see that day. They walked amongst his sculptured characters and 3D images depicting real life with a sense of irony and humor. Their favorite was called Subway where you could actually walk inside a subway car and sit next to the fantastical paper mache' figures looking just like people both of them had seen in real life. They giggled and laughed and it was just what they both needed.

Cara looked at Ginny who seemed even more radiant. She had cut her hair shorter. Maybe that was it, Cara thought.

They decided to go to Serendipity on East 60th, have a decadent dessert and continue their whimsical day.

The cold winter weather was taking a break and it was mild. It felt good walking crosstown and seeing children playing in the street. Couples laughed, grandparents enjoyed walking their grandchildren in strollers, and all enjoyed the surprisingly warm weather.

They arrived at Serendipity and since it was two in the afternoon, the wait wasn't long. Cara ordered the hot fudge sundae and Ginny the frozen hot chocolate.

"So, tell me how are things going with Jason?" Ginny asked, not wanting to mention Mel's illness. She knew it wasn't seeming good, and she wanted the conversation to be light. She sensed Cara needed that too.

"Jason's good. I think we're both ready to have this semester over. I'm looking forward to the summer," Cara said, taking a big spoonful of her sundae.

"I guess I should have asked how things are with the two of you. I know you just started seeing each other, but I think it's great the two of you got together. It's so romantic, especially since you were friends for such a long time. It sounds almost like a fairytale."

As Ginny spoke, Cara looked at Ginny and knew what she had known for a long time. She watched Ginny. Ginny's eyes were shining brightly and as she laughed, her head tilted gently back. Her big brown eyes looked up when she was remembering something. Cara watched as Ginny continued to talk, waving her hands expressively. moving her elegant slim fingers Ginny's long legs stretched out from under the table. Cara knew she felt more for Ginny than just friendship.

"Ginny, you look great with your new haircut and...hey are those new earrings?" Cara asked.

Ginny didn't answer right away. Instead, she touched her ears to feel her earrings and remembered the Tiffany gold post earrings with diamonds in the center that Jake had given her. She searched for something to say, mad at herself for forgetting to take them off and angry that she felt she had to lie.

"Oh these. I just found these at the bottom of my jewelry box." Sounding flustered and feeling her face getting flushed.

"Funny I don't remember you ever having those. They look expensive. They're beautiful."

Ginny tried to change the subject. "Did Jason follow up with everyone for the reunion with Matt and Lina?"

"He tried, but Lina has a tight schedule and Matt has been in London doing a semester abroad. I don't know, maybe Jason was right years ago when he said we will all move on." Cara said.

When they finished, Ginny headed to the train downtown and Cara walked to Madison Avenue to grab the bus uptown. As it rolled passed the expensive boutiques, Cara thought about all the items she would never be able to afford. Then the tone of the neighborhood changed as the bus turned West on 110th Street along Central Park, heading toward Broadway. The streets looked darker and the apartment buildings run down. When the bus reached Broadway, it changed again to the streets teaming with students.

Cara watched out the window at the couples holding hands, walking arm and arm, and even kissing. She was seeing Jason later, and felt a sadness wash over her.

Chapter Nineteen

Cara crossed Park Avenue with its tulip bulbs in the center island. The buds on the trees were about to burst and it was a beautiful day, but Cara didn't see it. She missed her fifth Avenue stop on the crosstown bus and had to walk back. She'd been doing that a lot lately. Her mind bounced around, unfocused. Cara walked into the Memorial Sloan Kettering lobby and headed to the elevator banks. She stood distracted until the "ding" announced the arrival of the elevator, she got in and pressed three.

When the elevator stopped at her floor a man asked, "Miss, is this your floor?"

She looked up and hurried off the elevator. She found the doctor's office and saw Connie and Mel in the waiting room. They both smiled when they saw her. She sat in the seat they saved for her next to Mel. She said nothing and stared off into space. Mel had gotten so thin. He reached over to Cara and took her hand reassuringly.

"Jacob" the nurse called out after half an hour. They all got up and followed the nurse to a small office where Dr. Andrew Katz was already sitting, looking very solemn.

Mel spoke first, "Dr. Katz, I just want you to know that I've decided that if the latest scans don't look good, I'm not going to have any more treatments. I don't want to continue to put myself or my family through more than we have to."

The doctor looked at Mel and then Connie and Cara.

"I completely understand. Well, the scans unfortunately do not show much improvement. We can wait a bit and see if you want to try..."

Mel cut him off, "Doctor, please just tell me what's next so I can be comfortable and not be a burden to my family. Tell me about hospice care."

The doctor explained some hospice options at home or at a hospital. Cara barely heard what was said.

Afterward they all left the hospital in silence.

Cara broke down outside the hospital building. Mel held her with his thin arms.

"Cara, please don't, you're upsetting your father," Connie said.

Cara ignored her and continued to hug her father until she composed herself.

The following day was Thursday. Cara met Jason in the Village in the afternoon, and they walked, then sat in Washington Square Park. He put his arm around her as she spoke about her father. Jason said he was there for her, and understood what she was going through. As they sat talking, the weather started to look overcast. They decided to find something hot to drink at a local cafe. Cara ordered hot chocolate, which reminded her of the afternoons that Mel would take her and Ginny to the Wollman Skating Rink in Central Park when they were small and they would all have hot chocolates. Cara looked at Jason. He was being so kind to her, just as Mel had always been, patient and understanding. Maybe she could grow to have more feelings for Jason, she thought. Maybe she wouldn't be living a lie. Maybe she could make this work with Jason. Cara smiled at him as he looked back at her. It was starting to drizzle. Cara said, "Let's go to your place."

Jason had just moved into a small studio on 12th Street. They bought a cheap umbrella at a corner newsstand and walked quickly to his apartment.

They walked up the four flights and then entered Jason's small studio. There were still moving boxes all about, but the bed was made. Cara needed to be held and touched to remove all the sadness she was feeling. She moved to the bed and started to undress. Jason came to her, kissed her gently and then undressed. He took her into his arms and they both made love for the first time.

Cara stayed close to home the next few months except to attend her classes. Her art was a comfort at this time. She escaped into her drawings and paintings and blocked out the world as she created. Her artwork became expressive, with bold shapes in her paintings and daring use of color in her illustrations.

The hospice nurse was coming every day now. Connie became impossible, snapping at Cara all the time. Cara did her best to tune her out, but she needed her mother right now, as she knew Connie needed her. The wall was up around Connie and Cara treaded lightly.

Mel died March 10th 1979.

Chapter Twenty

Jake's phone rang and he suspected it was Connie. He had spoken to Connie twice this week and she sounded scared. Jake never knew his sister to show any fear. He braced himself as he picked up the phone.

It was Cara.

"Uncle Jake...Dad passed away early this morning. I...just wanted you to know," Cara started sobbing.

"God Cara, I'm so sorry! I'll come over now. Is Connie there?"

"She can't talk. I'll tell her you're coming."

Jake told his co-workers what happened and left to head uptown.

Cara held her mother who cried in her arms. For weeks now, she thought that after her father passed away, she would leave home. Next semester she would be a college senior. She initially planned to live at home only her first year, but now, holding her mother in her arms, she thought otherwise. They would need each other this next year.

When a parent dies, the reality of mortality spits in your face. The finality that someone was here in your life, someone who shared every memory, every wonderful event, someone who was always there for you, has now disappeared forever. It was hard for Cara to accept. She kept expecting her father to be sitting in the living room or opening the refrigerator in the kitchen. Her father's absence filled her world.

Death happens and the world goes on. The garbage trucks still come in the morning, the baby still cries next door, the traffic still moves down Broadway. Cara felt as if she were moving in slow motion as the world zoomed by her. Why wasn't the world mourning alongside her?

Cara took care of organizing the catered lunch that would take place after the funeral that Sunday at their apartment. Connie made the funeral arrangements and let everyone know the date and time.

Cara found it difficult to deal with mundane things, such as the fact that she didn't own a black dress. She would have to shop for one and that was the last thing she wanted to do.

Why hadn't she bought one earlier? She knew this day was coming, she told herself, frustrated.

The Saturday of the funeral came. It was being held at the Ortiz RG Funeral Home on 72nd Street. Professors from Columbia University attended as well as Mel's students and friends. Family from Albany arrived the day before to spend time with Connie and Cara before the funeral.

Jake arrived early at the funeral home to make sure everything was set and greeted the family and friends as they arrived. Some he knew, but many he did not.

It was great to see that Mel had so many colleagues and friends who loved him. Jake wondered how many friends would actually show up to his funeral. He looked around, then saw her.

Ginny walked in looking like a beam of light in all this darkness. He walked up to her and kissed her on the cheek.

"How are you doing?" Ginny asked

"As well as expected. Are you good?" He asked, but before she could answer he looked away to greet another person who had just walked in. "Excuse me," Jake said as he turned away.

Ginny understood this must be a terrible day for everyone. She searched for Cara.

A minute later Ginny saw Jason and was relieved. They caught up and they stayed close to each other because neither knew anybody else at the funeral, except Connie, Cara and Jake.

Everyone took their seat. Then Connie rose to tell how she met Mel in Central Park twenty-seven years ago, when they both were having picnic lunches nearby each other. They spoke, and both knew immediately that they were right for each other. Connie got him out of his shell and Mel was a calming force for her. Connie said that she and Mel agreed, their greatest joy was when Cara was born. Mel would do absolutely anything for his little girl. Connie shared that Mel had told her just before he died that his life was filled with joy, and he was the luckiest man he knew.

Cara tried to speak, but it was difficult between her tears. She spoke of the days with her father when he took her hiking and boating, and how they loved to watch the tennis players. Then Cara said the most important thing Mel did for her was listen. He really listened to her. She said she always felt she could tell him anything. She would miss him terribly.

After the service everyone took taxis uptown for lunch at the apartment.

Jake took turns shaking hands and moving from person to person for hugs and quick remembrances of Mel. Jake looked dashing in his black suit. Ginny noticed some older women admiring him as he walked by.

As evening descended, Ginny felt in the way. Cara and Connie had family to speak to, and Jason was at her side. The same was true for Connie and Jake.

Ginny said her goodbyes and condolences. She looked for Jake, but he was engrossed in conversation with a colleague of Mel's. Her shyness took over. She felt awkward about interrupting him, and so she quietly left.

Chapter Twenty-One

Classes ended on Friday May 11 and finals were the following week. That Saturday Ginny and Jane were going to dinner with friends from school.

As they were going out Jane asked.

"Gin, just curious, why don't you see Jake on Saturdays? When I was dating Arnaud, Saturday was our date night. Usually Saturdays are spent with the person you're seeing."

"He's been busy with work and I guess he likes to spend Saturday working on his projects so Monday won't be too crazy," Ginny replied.

"I understand, I just hate to think there's another person who occupies his Saturdays. What about Sundays, can't he work then? Also have you spoken to Cara yet to tell her you are both seeing each other?" Jane asked.

"No, I felt it was his place to tell her," Ginny said.

"I don't know, Ginny."

As Ginny sat at dinner with Jane's school friends, she started to feel uncomfortable about the situation with Jake. Sure she wanted to see him Saturdays too. Sure, she wanted to meet his friends and have Cara and Connie know about their relationship. She had seen other women get clingy with guys they were seeing and it pushed them away. She knew Jake was very busy and in charge of a major account at a very prominent advertising company. He had huge responsibilities and a lot on his shoulders. The last thing this man needed was a silly college student who wanted more from him. She also needed her best friend to speak to, but couldn't. Why hadn't Jake mentioned anything to Cara? She also asked herself why she hadn't met any of Jake's friends. He didn't even mention friends. Then she realized that she didn't either. She told Jake about Jane because she would answer the phone sometimes at her apartment, but he never came upstairs to meet her.

Ginny and Jake had separate lives. How many people did they know outside of their time together?

During finals week she spoke to Cara and Cara asked her to come to Lake George after school classes were over.

"Cara, I'd love to. Let me see when my mother's coming to town and I'll let you know."

Ginny hadn't seen her mother since she visited for the holidays, back in December. She wished she could speak to her mother and sister about her personal life, but she never felt close to them. Her mother focused her questions about school, or what she planned for her future.

Jake came home from a business trip to Hong Kong on that Thursday and Ginny made plans to visit him Friday. They would order in since he said he would be exhausted and jet lagged.

"Why don't we see each other Saturday then?" Ginny asked.

"Unfortunately, I have notes I need to review for Monday, so Friday is best unless we hold off until next week?" he said.

"No, it was...I was just thinking of you," Ginny answered.

Ginny took the train to 86th and Lexington that Friday. She was happy that her finals had ended and she was looking forward to the summer.

She rode the elevator up to the tenth floor and buzzed Jake's apartment. He looked so fit and tan. He answered and immediately pulled her into his arms and kissed her.

"It is so wonderful to see you. I've really missed you. Maybe one time this summer you can join me on my trip and we can take a week or two traveling around Asia? Or we can take a shorter trip to an island somewhere."

"Oh Jake, that sounds wonderful! I missed you too, very much. It looks like you already had a sun-filled vacation. You are so tan," she said laughing.

"Come here beautiful." He said and he led her to the bedroom starting to undress her.

After making love he said. "Why don't I do my work reviews Fridays after work and this way we can see each other Saturday?"

"Oh, Jake, that would be great, but I don't want you to change your work routine for me. Whatever works for you."

"It's what I want to do. Consider it done,"

They ordered Chinese food and ate in bed before making love again.

The following day they went out for brunch and Ginny took the subway home, looking forward to telling Jane that she was wrong about Jake.

Still nothing was said about Cara.

Chapter Twenty-Two

Cara finished her classes and walked to meet Jason at his place. She had been struggling with what she knew was her reality. She faced the truth about herself when she saw Ginny at her father's funeral. Mel's passing was a wake-up call: don't hesitate to ask for what you want in life. Cara wanted to spend more time with Ginny on the day of the funeral, but with everything going on, she couldn't. She was hoping that Ginny would be able to accept her invite to Lake George soon. Cara was thinking that she might approach Ginny and talk to her gently about the feelings she'd had for her all these years. Then she'd talk herself out of it.

Cara thought it would destroy their friendship if Ginny didn't feel the same way.

She would lie in bed at night going over and over what she would say and how she would approach the subject.

Maybe Ginny felt the same way after all. Ginny hasn't had a boyfriend even throughout college.

One thing she had to deal with now was Jason. She could not continue to make love to him feeling nothing. Every time she thought about it, she couldn't help but feel that she would be hurting him so much, so she avoided the subject, but now she was making excuses to not go to bed.

Cara headed to Jason's studio apartment. She climbed the stairs and when Jason answered the door, he went to kiss her. She kissed him quickly and went to the fabric couch that was way too big for the room. He sat next to her and she turned to face him and took his hands.

"Jason, I need to talk to you," Cara said as she sat down.

"Cara, please don't do "The Talk", Jason said standing up. "I'm not stupid, I've known something has not been right for a while. It's like you recoil when I come to you. I don't know what's wrong," he continued.

"I don't know either, but it's something I have to deal with by myself."

"I don't understand Cara."

She stood up to stand next to him, and moved in to hug him. At first, he didn't hug back, but finally he did and they held each other for a long time.

The next day, Ginny called Cara.

"I was thinking of when to come to Lake George. How does mid-June sound?" Ginny asked.

"Why don't you come Memorial Day weekend and stay the week?" Cara offered.

"I can't, I'm busy that weekend, but I'm looking forward to spending time with you away from the city."

"Ok, busy girl. So, let's plan the weekend of June 15. Think about staying for a week if you want. My mother may stay in the city part of that time, so we can have the whole house to ourselves."

"I will, Cara. Thank you. I'm looking forward to it."

Cara hung up excited with her heart beating faster. This would be the chance to come clean with her feelings for Ginny. She would ask her mother to let her have the house to herself. She would tell Connie that it may be the last summer that she and Ginny would have alone time up there, since they both would be graduating from college next year and who knows where they'll be after that.

Chapter Twenty-Three

Jake had never moved a day around to please a woman before, only himself. Was this a change happening? Could he be starting to fall for her?

He mentioned the date change to Iris who seemed okay with switching. She told him she would then sign up to teach a yoga class on Saturdays so it worked out.

He wasn't ready to give up Iris yet. The sexual sync was still there. It did feel good to be teaching Ginny things, things he would try with Iris, but Ginny was still timid, although it was becoming exciting to see her open up since he first touched her, and discover herself with him.

A trip to Hong Kong was coming up in the summer and even though he mentioned it to Ginny he decided that maybe St. John or St. Martin would be a better start. The memories of that trip to St. John with Amanda were long gone. He started to fantasize about the places he would take Ginny and all those nights in bed.

Then his thought about his last business trips to Hong Kong. He enjoyed his nights there too. One of his male colleagues named Lucas took him to a "Villa" on his first business trip. Villas were basically brothels scattered around different neighborhoods all over Kowloon and Hong Kong Island. The girls who worked there usually came from poor farming backgrounds where their families were more than happy to have their daughter go to a city to make money and send back money to them. Besides it was also one less mouth to feed.

The Madame or Sir would pleasantly greet the men when they arrived and then the girls were introduced. Drinks were offered and they were expensive, twice the usual price at a bar, but no one cared. One could lounge for a bit talking to the girls available and once one was chosen, the men would be led by the chosen girl to a room. Condoms were shown as an option, but not required. The young girls at Jake's favorite Villa were as young as fifteen and already "trained". If the Villa got to know you, for an up charge, you could have a girl come to your hotel which could be more convenient for traveling business men. Jake was staying at the Regent on the bay in Kowloon. He made a point of tipping the head concierge so that his "visitor" was not stopped and allowed up to his room. This practice was what made him pause to bring Ginny. He began to like his trips to this part of the world alone.

When Jake returned to his East Side neighborhood in New York City after his business trips abroad, it would take him a few days to adjust to the time change, and an environment so completely different from his time in Asia.

When home, Jake loved to walk around Madison Avenue to look at the boutiques and shop for a gift for Ginny or Iris, and for himself too. Then he would turn East to Park Avenue to look at the luxury pre-war buildings that framed the tree lined avenue. He would walk a while looking at the rich well-dressed people on the street and he knew that he had arrived living amongst them. He looked at the women on the arms of these wealthy men. They wore the finest clothing with style and grace. He knew they went to the finest schools and came from blue blood backgrounds.

The twenty plus year age difference between him and Ginny didn't matter here, as he viewed older men with their younger wives.

As he kept walking, he started to feel like a nouveau riche character in a movie who didn't quite fit in, but he would show them that he belonged. He turned again and this time walked west. He now crossed Park Avenue, then Madison

Avenue and stopped on Fifth Avenue to gaze at his goal. This was where he wanted to live, across from Central Park in a three-bedroom showcase above the treeline.

He would make sure that the woman on his arm fit that image too.

Iris was not an option with her bohemian ways. Yes she was beautiful, but her style and manner didn't work in this world.

Ginny was another story. She was young and gorgeous. Her style was not fixed yet. She had not discovered her stride. He could mold her into the image that would fit perfectly into his world on Fifth Avenue amongst the wealthiest in New York City.

He would see where his relationship with Ginny continued to go and then talk to Connie and Cara about it. That would bring their love to a whole new level. He knew that Ginny had not said anything about their relationship yet because Cara would have called him. He knew in his heart when the right time came, all would work out and Cara and Connie would be happy for both of them.

Chapter Twenty-Four

Ginny felt like skipping down the street. She was so happy. Jake had asked her to join him for a vacation in St. Martin for Memorial Day weekend and into the following week. He told her that on Saturday he would take her shopping for clothes for the trip. He had booked La Samanna, the resort hotel and spa. He had also booked massages and other luxurious treatments for them. She felt that Jake and she were a real couple moving forward to something serious. Maybe she would talk to her mother about it in July when she visited, if the conversation allowed.

She didn't know what to say when Cara asked about seeing her Memorial Day weekend. Saying she was busy was the truth and she'd have to figure out something to say if she asked what she did.

She exited the subway at 86th Street and walked east to Jake's apartment where he was all ready to step out to take her shopping. They headed to Madison Avenue where he took her to buy three sundresses, two pairs of sandals, three bathing suits, two beach coverups, and a wide brimmed sun hat. Every salesperson looked admiringly at the beautiful couple as they rang up their expensive sale.

There were so many bags when they were finished that they had to take a taxi the six blocks back to Jake's apartment building where the doorman then took the bundles.

Ginny then modeled everything again in the living room when they returned to his place. Jake sat on his couch looking so pleased with the way she looked in each outfit.

After the last dress was put on and modeled he pulled her to him and told her how beautiful she was and how proud he was to be with her. She blushed and thanked him for all the gifts.

"I have an idea, why don't you pick one to wear to dinner tonight. It's warm out and we'll go to Orsay," Jake said to her.

"Oh, I'd love that Jake," Ginny said and couldn't help jumping up and down like a little kid. She hadn't heard Jake say, "I love you" yet, but it sure felt as though he had.

Their trip was now a week away and Ginny avoided calling Cara. She was home alone one evening when she knew Jake was at a dinner meeting and the phone rang. Maybe it was for Jane, but they would call back, then again maybe it was Cara and she just wanted to avoid having to explain where she was going on vacation and lie. She didn't answer the phone.

Then Ginny thought, I'll ask Jane if she'll be okay with me telling Cara that I'll be going upstate with her or someplace else with her for a week. Yes, that would work, she said to herself.

That evening Jane came home and they both ordered Chinese food for dinner and were sitting around, talking about summer plans. Jane was going to work at Tower Records, which she was thrilled about because of the employee discount.

Ginny had not made plans to work that summer. Her mother had been pushing her to get a job, but she wasn't motivated.

After dinner Ginny asked Jane, "I have a favor to ask. Would you be okay if I said to Cara that I'm with you for Memorial Day weekend and the following week? I would say we were going upstate somewhere."

Jane gave Ginny an inquisitive look. "Gin, why in the world would you want to do that?"

"Because, I'm going away with Jake and Cara doesn't know. We haven't told her anything about us yet."

"Why not?" Jane asked.

Ginny's shoulders slumped. She didn't know what to say. Jane was right, why not. She wanted to get angry at Jane. She was just asking a small favor, why couldn't she just agree to help her? It wasn't really a big deal.

"Look I don't know, but right now nothing has been said, so until it is I was wondering if you could..."

"Participate in a lie to your best friend?" Jane said sarcastically.

"Okay, you've made your point Jane," Ginny said.

"Gin, I'll do it this one time, only because I'm not close to Cara and this may be moot since I don't see her much, but I'm not comfortable doing this. It seems so important to you, so as your friend I'll help you, but only this once, agreed?"

"Agreed," Ginny said softly.

Jake picked Ginny up the following week with the car service and they headed to the airport. Ginny was happy to be going on this beautiful vacation and was trying to put aside the reality that the only person who knew where she was going and with whom was her roommate Jane.

They arrived at La Samanna with warm weather and crystal blue skies. The first afternoon after they arrived, they relaxed by the beach, having cocktails and oysters before dinner. Before going out Jake had picked out what dress and sandals he wanted Ginny to wear. He even suggested that she should wear her hair down with that dress. At dinner they had a sumptuous seafood platter on the hotel's veranda overlooking the sea. Ginny felt like a princess. She didn't mind having her prince tell her how to dress. After all, he was more experienced with what styles looked good for certain occasions.

The rest of the week they took hired cars with drivers to different towns and beaches for the day. One of her favorite times was when they went to the French side of the island to eat lobsters on the beach. She was surprised when Jake commented that it wasn't that upscale enough for him and he preferred eating in a restaurant than at this small "shack" on the beach. Ginny didn't say anything, but kept enjoying her lobster lunch. Maybe over time with her, Jake would loosen up and also enjoy simple things, she told herself.

Toward the end of the trip, Jake seemed to be getting antsy. They had massages in the morning, but then Jake wanted to take a tennis lesson. The next day Ginny wanted to relax by the pool with him, but he said he wanted to go to town and look at some galleries. She let him go on his own. She worried about the stress he had because she knew he was on blood pressure medication and his doctor wanted to put him on something else for his cholesterol. He said he had a friend who was giving him some herbal supplements for that so not to worry. She hoped to meet this friend.

Their last night was spent at a beautiful restaurant in town, but Jake didn't like the lighting and complained about the service. He also looked at Ginny over dinner and told her that her hair should have been worn up with this dress.

Ginny kept telling herself that poor Jake must have been so stressed to be away with all the responsibilities of the new position at work. She wished she could do or say something to ease his stress.

They flew back home with Jake sleeping through most of the flight.

Chapter Twenty-Five

Connie agreed to stay home in New York City for the weekend of June 15, when Cara said Ginny would be visiting. She knew Cara wanted to spend time with Ginny as it might be one of their last summers as non-working, single girls. She was hoping Cara's relationship with Jason would work out. She worried about Cara losing her father; a father with whom she was so close. And Cara hadn't met many new friends at school. Maybe because she was living at home? Maybe this summer Cara would meet someone special.

Cara spent time working on drawings for her portfolio, which was quite extensive by now. One of her professors had suggested interning in the art department at an ad agency this summer. She thought of asking Jake about internships at Benton & Bowles, but she really wanted a carefree summer. She listed herself as a babysitter on several job boards around Columbia and Barnard campuses. That she could do easily while keeping her days free.

The timing to go to Lake George with Ginny at the end of the week hadn't been confirmed yet. Cara tried to call Ginny several times the week before she left on her vacation, but there was never an answer, so at the end of the week, she tried calling again. The phone rang for a while and as she was preparing to hang up, Jane answered.

"Hi Jane, this is Cara, is Ginny there?"

"Hi Cara. No Ginny's out, I'll tell her you called." Jane said quickly, trying to get off the phone, not wanting Cara to ask any questions about the vacation she and Ginny were supposed to have gone on. She wasn't sure what Ginny had even told Cara yet.

"Ok thanks." Cara said and hung up looking at the phone. She wanted to ask Jane if Ginny was back from her trip and where she went. God, Jane can be rather abrupt. She realized she didn't even know where Ginny had gone on vacation, or with whom. That night she did not get a return call from Ginny.

Cara went grocery shopping with Connie that evening. She was sure her mother asked her along to carry the packages. She didn't mind though. She and Connie were getting along well these days since Mel had passed. Cara saw her mother's vulnerability, and also her fierceness, as her way of showing love. She understood that her need for perfection was also a need to make everything okay. Cara was slowly under-standing her mother. She was also sorry for her because Jake wasn't coming around much these days. She knew about the promotion and concluded he must be so busy, but she missed her Uncle Jake and so did Connie.

When they came home from shopping the phone was ring-ing. Connie asked Cara to get it while she put the groceries away.

"Hello?" Cara asked.

"Cara, it's me. Sorry I missed your call last night," Ginny said.

"I called to work out our timing for this coming weekend and also to ask about your trip. I don't even know where you went," Cara said, chuckling.

"Oh, it was great, I went upstate to the Catskills area," Ginny said.

"Sounds relaxing. What town did you visit?" Cara asked.

"I forget, but it was really relaxing."

"That's good, did you go with school friends?"

"Umm yes, with Jane," Ginny replied.

"Really? Jane's so weird, why didn't she say anything when I called?"

"Oh, who knows, maybe she was just tired from the drive home."

"Yes, I'm sure. So let's plan on Friday driving up to Lake George. Can you stay the week?"

"Gosh Cara, because I've just been away I don't think so, but I can stay until Monday if that's alright."

"Oh Ginny, I'm sorry about that, I was hoping for more time with you. I understand though. Okay then, come by here early, maybe around two o' clock after lunch then we'll drive up," Cara said.

"Sounds good. I'll see you then!" Ginny answered.

Cara hung up thinking something seemed wrong, but she didn't want to deal with it. She wanted to focus on the days she would have with Ginny.

Chapter Twenty-Six

Jake was relieved to be home from his vacation. He unpacked his bag after arriving at his apartment and poured himself a vodka. His apartment was clean and in order since his cleaning lady came while he was away. He walked to the black leather couch and sat down and sipped his drink.

The vacation was terrific and Ginny was easy going. All she seemed to want to do was to make him happy. She looked beautiful in her dresses, but needed some styling help with her hair and jewelry, which she would learn, he was sure, over time. The vacation resort was exactly what he wanted with a beach on the property, a pool when you didn't want sand, tennis courts, an amazing restaurant, and a romantic bedroom suite for Ginny and him to enjoy. So why did he need to spend time alone when they were away?

Jake got up to pour a second vodka and boiled water to make pasta. After the pasta was done, he poured hot tomato sauce over it, walked back to his couch, and turned on the TV. He decided to watch an old movie.

The movie was *Pygmalion,* starring Leslie Howard. He watched the story of a linguistics professor boasting that he could take a young cockney girl and pass her off as a princess after properly teaching her. As Jake watched he began to feel like professor Henry Higgins shaping and molding his own Eliza Doolittle. Was that what he was doing with Ginny? Ginny was from the Upper West Side of Manhattan, from a middle-class family, divorced parents and a father who almost never visited. She didn't come from the blue-blooded upbringing and schooling of his new neighborhood of the East Side.

Everything was new to Ginny, the restaurants, the luxury boutiques, the lavish vacations, all of which she had never experienced before. Yes, it was marvelous to introduce her to these things. He felt some power in doing that. She would never experience anything close to what he had shown her with those silly young school boys at NYU.

He felt proud that he could do that for her, and yet...would her lack of sophistication and worldly experience be obvious to people, especially the ones he hoped to meet in the world he was imagining? Of course, he came from that same upbringing as Ginny, but he had surpassed that, and moved on through hard work and his financial success. Jake always made sure to read the latest new book, attend the newest gallery and visit important museum exhibits. He would make sure to see an opera each season and read the reviews to know what the critics thought. He read up on what were considered good vintages of both red and white wines, and what clothing designer labels were important at the moment. He knew he could turn on his charm and fit into a circle of society. Could she? Or would they see her unsophisticated background through the clothes he bought her?

Ginny was so sweet he thought and so eager to learn. She listened intently to things he said. She seemed like a sponge taking everything in. She nodded and agreed with his opinions on everything from the artwork they just saw, the music they listened to, and the political opinions he voiced.

But what was her opinion? It was charming to see someone grow up and blossom, but when would she be her own woman with thoughts and opinions of her own? When would she say what she wanted to wear, what she wanted to eat and what was her favorite restaurant, which artists she admired and which artists she just didn't care for, and when would she argue with him over a difference of opinion?

Of course, he then thought, would he really want that?

Chapter Twenty-Seven

Ginny took the Broadway subway uptown that Friday afternoon to meet Cara on 112th Street and Riverside Drive. This was where Cara told Ginny that Connie had parked the car the night before, after the ritual of circling for alternate side street parking.

Ginny was looking forward to spending time with Cara. They hadn't seen much of each other since Mel's funeral.

She wanted to share with Cara the change in her life, that she had found someone that she loved deeply. She was walking on air all the time. Of course, she couldn't say it was Jake. She thought perhaps of saying it was someone at school. Maybe one of Jane's friends? Oh no that wouldn't do, Jane would kill her for having her name in another lie. She decided to play it by ear and see how the conversation went this weekend.

The drive up to Lake George was beautiful. The trees were in their full burst of green and it was early enough in the day that there was no traffic. They decided to stop in Saratoga Springs for an early dinner. They drove through the center on Main Street, and parked to find a place to grab a meal. Cara said that she and Connie had tried this small place called Eddie's and it was pretty good and it had reasonable prices. Ginny looked across the street at the Olde Bryan Inn restaurant. It looked as if it had been there forever. She was sure dinner would be very expensive at that elegant Inn. Jake probably knew about it and maybe they would go one day when they would be making this trip together.

As they approached Glen Lake Road to the large log cabin Ginny felt nostalgic for the days when Cara and she spent summers there as children. She also remembered Jake's presence when she was a child. He would take Cara and her out in the row boat onto the lake and sometimes they even tried to fish. She remembered how much fun he was sometimes pretending that he saw dolphins on the lake. Then they would go to Calves Pen where Jake and Connie jumped into the water from rock cliffs. He made them laugh all the time, playing games such as hide and seek outside before dinner, and after dinner board games like Chutes and Ladders or Life. As they got older the games became chess which Cara played or scrabble which Mel joined in for. She also recalled the fun Cara and she had giggling at night and having their sleepovers in one room. They would sneak snacks into the room and make sure to clean up everything in the morning to avoid Connie scolding Cara.

The car pulled up to the house and they brought their bags in.

"Just put your bags down and you can choose a room later," Cara said as they walked in. Ginny wondered why she said that since she always stayed in the small room on the left upstairs for many years now.

Ginny walked to the picture window that looked out onto the lake. The lake was shimmering as the sun set and she looked at the orange ball going down over the horizon.

"Ginny, I brought a pie for dessert and I think Connie left some ice cream for us. And...I also brought this!" Cara announced as she reached into her backpack and pulled out a bottle of champagne.

"Wow, great, what's the occasion?" Ginny asked, smiling.

"I thought we'd celebrate the summer, heading into our final year, and our special friendship all these years." Cara said as she put the champagne in the freezer to chill.

She then put a Joni Mitchell record on the turntable in the living room.

They both sat around the living room talking about Connie and how Cara felt their relationship was improving. Ginny said that she would take clues from her with her own mother who was visiting soon.

Cara stood up and went to the kitchen to get the apple pie and ice cream and took the champagne out of the freezer. She popped the bottle and poured the champagne into the fluted glasses. Ginny helped her bring everything to the coffee table by the couch.

Cara was feeling nervous about how she would bring up her feelings for Ginny. She thought she'd ask her about her trip first to ease her nerves.

"So tell me more about your trip with Jane in the Catskills," Cara said.

"It was good, we stayed at a small hotel in Saugerties. Funny that I had trouble remembering that name before. Then we spent some time going around Woodstock. The stores were so much fun, looking like they were just stuck in the 60s. So we just had a good time visiting the area. Jane has become a good friend. I'm glad she's my roommate." Ginny trailed off not knowing what else she could make up.

"You must have been doing a lot outdoors. You look so tan!" Cara said smiling.

Ginny then asked about Jason.

"How is Jason? Are you going to have him up here this summer?"

"No Ginny. Actually, we broke up. I was trying to figure out why it wasn't working for a while. Jason is such a great guy, but for someone else. It was difficult for me to end it with him. I've been doing some self-reflection, and I think I know what will make me happy."

Cara was wondering if this was the right time to say something to her. She felt so tongue tied. Cara sat up and finally braced to speak about her feelings when Ginny spoke.

"I'm so sorry Cara to hear about you and Jason, but I can understand. It's so hard to find someone special who you know is right for you."

Ginny was quiet then continued.

"Cara, I have to tell you something…I started seeing someone who I think is very special. He's older than me and I met him at a deli of all places, downtown. We've seen each other a few times and I really like him," Ginny said thinking one day they will have a laugh about this. She told herself she's not lying after all. Everything she said so far about this at least was true.

"Really. That's amazing. I'm so happy for you," Cara said, trying desperately to hide her shock and disappointment. When in the world did this happen?

"What's his name?" Cara asked.

"Gene" Ginny finally found her lie. She wasn't even sure how she came up with that name.

"Is it serious?"

"Actually I think so, but we'll see," Ginny said beaming, looking so happy.

Then Ginny said, "I'm sorry to just be speaking about myself. You said you think you know what will make you happy with someone. Please tell me what you think that would be."

"Oh, I'm really not sure. I'll figure it out." Cara said, feeling like she was going to cry.

"Oh Cara, you will find your love, I know you will."

"Yes, sorry to seem weird. I'm so happy for you Ginny."

Cara then made the excuse that she was tired from the long drive and went to bed early telling Ginny to make herself at home and to feel free to take the bedroom on the left that she always stayed in.

On Saturday, after they had breakfast, they went for a hike on a trail nearby that Mel used to take them on. That night they went to Vincent's for dinner in town where they remembered sharing a steak when they were little because the portion was so generous. When it came to dessert though, they each had their own.

On Sunday, Cara and Ginny took the rowboat out and enjoyed the serene view around the lake as it seemed to sparkle in the sun. In the evening they cooked chicken breasts on the grill with salad and potatoes. They spoke about their goals for when they graduated next year and of their high school friends who seemed to be moving on. They promised each other that this would never happen to them.

On Monday, around noon, Cara drove Ginny to Fort Edward for the Amtrak train back to New York City.

As Cara drove back to the cabin, the sky started to darken and she could see lightning flash ahead of her. It suddenly started to rain and it was coming down hard. She pulled over to the side of the road to wait it out.

She sat in her car and quietly cried.

Chapter Twenty-Eight

The car service was stuck in traffic going across town. Jake was getting antsy. He tried to relax by looking at the Travel and Leisure magazine in the seat pocket in front of him. He was headed to a business dinner at Mr. Chows on East 57th Street. A bunch of his associates were getting together to discuss new strategies for clients using television advertising. He thought that there would be some business discussed, but mainly a lot of eating and drinking, all on the expense account.

When he arrived all the guys and the one woman associate invited were at the round table in the back. He liked this place and loved gazing at the celebrities and models that frequently went there, but since he was late unfortunately his seat was facing inward, not out where he could glance at the view.

Network station prime time fees had gone up significantly and they spoke of the advantages and disadvantages of taking shorter time slots. They also spoke about the new magazines that had emerged where some products could be featured.

When the food came, they all passed the entrees around for everyone to share and ordered second drinks. Jake was sitting next to Stewart who was a new guy in their department. He was younger than Jake and single. Jake leaned in and said to Stewart that they should go to the bar after dinner and order an after-dinner drink and enjoy the view of the models who usually come in late. Stewart readily agreed.

When dinner was over, Jake told them he was going to stick around a bit and have a nightcap. Stewart joined him as the others smiled and joked that they better not see them in the same clothes at work in the morning.

The bar started to get full and feel like a party. Jake was in his element now. He turned on the charm with women and men around him holding court in the small group. Two blonde beauties wearing dresses that seemed to be poured onto their bodies came up to them to order drinks. Jake spoke with one of them and then offered to buy them both a drink. Stewart was clearly getting drunk and having a great time. Jake could hold his liquor and carried most of the conversation.

More people gathered around and everyone was speaking about the best vacations they had, where the best luxury real estate around the world was and where the stock market was headed. Around midnight, Stewart said he was heading home. Jake excused himself and took Stewart outside to put him into a taxi. Jake returned back to the bar area and chatted more with the taller of the two blondes in the group touching her on her shoulder as he leaned in. At one point she looked at Jake to tell him that she lived nearby and asked if he wanted to come over.

"I don't usually go to the homes of beautiful women I just met, but you are very convincing so...yes let's go," Jake said, laughing and steadying himself. He lost track of how many vodkas he had.

It was warm out and Jake was able to clear his head as they walked the two blocks to her modern apartment building on First Avenue. The doorman nodded to her as he held the door open for them. They rode the elevator up to the twelfth floor. When he stepped off the elevator the hallways looked like some of the fine hotels that Jake had stayed in when he traveled. She must do very well with whatever it is she does, he thought. He made a mental note to ask her tonight what exactly she did for a living. Maybe she's from one of those wealthy families that usually lives around here and doesn't need to work, he thought.

When they entered her apartment, she put down her purse onto the table near the front door entrance. He looked around and it looked expensively furnished. He was sure she came from money.

She then turned to him and said, "Ok darling, let's get the business out of the way. I charge five hundred dollars for the evening. If you are planning on sleeping over, it's a thousand. Payable up front. I take cash or checks with two forms of ID. We can start right away after this is settled."

Jake stepped back and looked at her in shock. "What the fuck! I...I don't do this. I have no trouble getting women in this town. This is not what I need or want. You deceived me. I can't believe I fell for this. Jesus, I'm leaving."

"That's fine darling, there's no loss on my end, but you.re deluding yourself if you didn't know what the score is. It's fine, just leave now."

Jake opened the door thinking if he were a different man, he could have raped her or worse. Why didn't she say something on the way over? Did she think once I was in her place, I'd be embarrassed, or too excited to leave?

He walked five blocks before hailing a taxi uptown.

When he got home it was one o'clock in the morning and he was still awake and aroused. He called Iris.

Chapter Twenty-Nine

Cara called her mother to ask if she wouldn't mind taking the train up to Lake George instead of her bringing the car back to the city. Cara had originally planned to return and stay in New York for July and part of August, but now changed her mind. She wanted to stay for the summer. It would be the last time she would be able to do this. Next year she hoped she would be working. Connie asked Cara if everything was all right? Cara replied that she wanted to work on her portfolio in a quieter environment and felt it was perfect if she stayed in Lake George.

Cara found she liked and even needed solitude. At first she was afraid that she'd get lonely, but it was good to have that alone time. Connie still came up on Fridays by train and went home on Monday morning back to New York. During the week was Cara's time, and she relished it.

Cara worked on drawings of scenes around the lake, and also of the cabin, working carefully to get all the details right. Early one morning she decided to do a self-portrait. She had never done one before. She took her time studying her face. Her blue eyes were evenly set. Her nose was petite like her mother's and she got her full lips from Mel. She wore her red hair down for the portrait and liked the way the curls framed her face. She didn't see that crazy wild mane she hated growing up. As she studied herself, she decided she didn't mind the way she looked. She never considered herself pretty, but she wasn't bad looking after all, she thought.

Cara was feeling good about herself now. She knew it would take time to be comfortable with who she was and to be honest with herself. She thought of Ginny. She was glad that she didn't get a chance to say anything. They had a special friendship that would have been terrible to destroy.

One night she was in the living room and she saw on the very bottom of the large bookcase an old photo album. It was from when her mother was little. She remembered seeing it many years ago when she was young, but hadn't bothered to look at it since. As she flipped through the pages, she saw her grandparents whom she had never met, smiling with a baby in their arms and a little girl about six years old. The photos showed her mother and her Uncle Jake growing up year after year as she turned the pages. Connie was always a little itty bitty girl, but Jake started to fill out when he was about six and was actually fat even into his teenage years. There were some school portrait photos that her grandparents must have prized when they were taken because so many were in the photo album. Her mother was there with her beautiful red hair and small features. The photos of Jake as a teenager showed an unhappy boy with curly brown hair who was overweight skin breaking out. In his high school graduation photo, he wasn't even smiling. Poor Uncle Jake, she thought. That must have been hard for him. As she continued to flip the pages it showed Jake getting slimmer in his twenties and becoming the handsome man he is today. She smiled and put the album away.

Connie came up on a Friday mid-August, planned to stay two weeks and return right after Labor Day. Cara met her at the train station and they went right out for dinner. Connie was just starting to allow herself go out and enjoy herself a bit since Mel passed away. Most of the family lived in either Albany or in San Francisco so the shoulder to lean on was Cara's.

On some days Cara and Connie would pack sandwiches and take the boat out and enjoy the peacefulness of the lake. On other days, Cara would be working on a drawing while Connie read or they would go out for a hike on Mel's trail.

One night Cara said to Connie, "Mom, I pulled out the old photo album. It's been years since I looked at it. You were so adorable as a child, but poor Uncle Jake. He must have had a hard time with his weight problem. God, you wouldn't think it was the same person now."

"Cara, you don't know the half of it. He wouldn't want to go to school sometimes because he got teased so much, even by the girls. Then in high school when kids start to date, he would rush home from school and shut his door and read. It was only in his Freshman year at college that he started to get tall and his face cleared up. He had so many years of feeling insecure that when he started dating and going out, he serial dated. That's when I started teasing him about that, which I shouldn't have really. He was just trying to figure out which girls he liked, that's all."

"Kids can be so cruel. He's made up for his insecurities, big time. He's overflowing with self-confidence now!" Cara said.

"I don't know about that. Sometimes those things stay with you."

That night they grilled steaks and played scrabble and watched a movie together. It was peaceful. Cara hadn't felt this good to be with her mother in a long time. They were getting along so well.

One day they went to Calves Pen where Connie and Jake used to love to go as kids. She told Cara how frightened Jake was of jumping in the water there. The other kids used to be so mean to him, teasing him about jumping in and making a big splash.

"Jake was really a fragile child, but as he got older he gained some confidence, thank God." Connie said. She was opening up to her as she hadn't done in the past.

Cara felt close to her mother now and a discussion came up about how special Jason was. Cara said that Jason was great in so many ways, but he just wasn't right for her. Connie told her that she would find a nice young man one day, maybe through someone at work or through friends.

Cara felt she now had the confidence to say, "Mom, I need to talk to you about something."

Chapter Thirty

On Thursday August 23rd Ginny woke up exhausted. She hadn't slept well. She was having some nausea all night from what she thought was her dinner. Her mother was coming to visit from California that weekend to spend time with her and Sara, and the last thing she wanted was to be sick.

By noon that day she was feeling better and was relieved.

She would miss her Saturday with Jake this week because there was a dinner planned with her mother, sister and her sister's boyfriend, Adrian. When she told Jake about it, she was hoping he would say he'd love to join, but instead he told her he hoped she would have a good time.

Ginny's mother Barbara was staying at the Hilton Hotel in midtown Manhattan. Barbara was a beautiful woman who was also fragile. She had endured years of emotional abuse from Ginny's father Peter, but she held onto the fantasy that they could work things out. She held off signing divorce papers for seven years and finally did when Ginny was thir-teen. She had toughened up since then, but did not get into another relationship.

Peter sometimes showed up for graduations and a few birth-days, but as Sara and Ginny grew older, they didn't care if he came to visit or not. Sara reacted to their parent's bad marriage by being headstrong. Ginny on the other hand was naturally shy and as a child, retreated inward even more. Her friendship with Cara and Cara's family helped her come out of her shell and she gained some confidence. As she grew older, Ginny had no example of a good relationship or a good male role model except for Mel and Connie. Cara's family was the family she wanted.

Ginny went to the Hilton hotel that Saturday. Her mother hugged when she opened her hotel room door.

"My goodness Ginny, you look great hon!" Barbara said, as she looked her daughter over. She noticed Ginny's dress looked expensive. Barbara gave Ginny a small allowance dur-ing the school year so she wondered how she could afford it.

They chatted a bit about Sara and her boyfriend Adrian. Barbara thought they were going to get engaged. Then her mother asked, "How about you Ginny, are you seeing any-one?"

Ginny was surprised that she even asked.

"Actually, yes," Ginny said, sick of lying and keeping her relationship with Jake hidden. Besides, her mother might be happy. She knew Jake from when Ginny was little and he'd come to visit Cara's family.

"Well it's kind of a funny story, I ran into Jake, Cara's uncle last year before the holidays near NYU and we went out to dinner, and well, things just progressed..." Ginny said smiling.

"Are you serious? You are seeing Jake Baines? How do Cara and Connie feel about this?" Barbara asked, turning and looking at her.

"They don't know yet. Jake just wanted to wait a while to tell them. I'm so happy mom. He treats me so well," Ginny gushed.

"Sorry, I'm a bit stunned. He's more than twice your age. Yes, he's a charming guy but, I don't know," Barbara said.

"Don't know what?" Ginny said, annoyed.

"Ginny, just take it slowly with him, okay please?"

"Fine. I'm happy and just wanted to share it," Ginny said, turning her head to look out the window.

"Understood, okay let's drop it. Let me fix my hair and then we'll meet Sara and Adrian."

Ginny sat on the bed as her mother went to the bathroom. She wanted her mother to be happy for her and to embrace her relationship. Her mother was thrilled for Sara when she met Adrian. She started to feel angry and felt that her mother didn't acknowledge important events in her life.

Dinner conversation was focused on Sara and her new job. Ginny was now sullen and didn't say much.

Barbara stayed the weekend, spending time with friends to catch up and saw Sara again for breakfast before leaving that Monday. She only spoke to Ginny once more before leaving to go back to California.

That week Ginny's nausea occurred several times sporadically and she started to get concerned. She hadn't eaten anything that could have caused this. She decided to see the school nurse and get it checked out. The nurse took blood and felt her stomach.

"It doesn't seem to be anything serious or you would be in pain. It could be stress related, but I'll run some tests. The results should come back in a couple days, and some may come as soon as tomorrow and we'll call you," The nurse said

Stress? Ginny thought, why in the world would it be stress? I'm happy. I'm in love. It's summertime.

The following day, she and Jane went to Central Park to sit on the Great Lawn, and she told Jane about the visit with her mother and that she had told her mother about Jake.

"Is she now only the second person besides me who knows about your relationship?" Jane asked.

"Yes, but it's complicated. My mother expressed concern, but she knows I'm happy."

"Ginny, do you think it is normal that Jake won't say anything about your relationship to friends or family? Have you ever met any of his friends?"

"Jane, I'm sure he will let everyone know in time. It was awkward at first and now I guess he wants to see where it goes."

"See where it goes? You just told me you're in love." Jane said, looking at Ginny.

"God, I don't know. Okay, I'll speak to him."

They stayed in the park until three in the afternoon. Ginny returned to their apartment to work on a short article on growing up in Manhattan that she would submit to a local magazine or paper.

When she put the key in the door to her apartment, she could hear the phone ringing. She rushed to pick it up thinking it was Jake.

"Hello?" Ginny asked happily.

"Is this Ginny Harris?"

"Yes it is," Ginny answered, puzzled.

"This is the nurse's office at NYU. We have the results of your blood test. Everything is normal which is great. We did however find out the probable cause of your nausea. You're pregnant."

Chapter Thirty-One

It was Friday and Jake left work early as he usually did in the summer. He decided to walk slowly through Central Park uptown zig zagging through the streets uptown following the green lights. He was seeing Iris tonight and they were going to the Metropolitan Museum to see a new exhibit of Impressionist art, then to dinner. When he got home, he showered and changed and was getting ready to meet Iris when the phone rang.

It was Ginny.

"Jake, I know you're busy working on a project tonight for work and don't like to be disturbed, but I have to talk to you."

"Ginny? Sweetheart, I'm right in the middle of something important. I really can't talk now. I'm on a deadline. I'll call you tomorrow and we will see each other then. I've got to go now," and he hung up.

Ginny put the phone down. She didn't know what to do. She sat on the couch and stared off into space.

"Hey Gin, what do you want for dinner, should we just order pizza or maybe Chinese?"

Ginny didn't even hear Jane open the front door.

Jane took one look at her and said, "Ginny, what's wrong? You look terrible!"

"I was feeling nauseous these last several days and went to the school nurse. I'm pregnant Jane. I just don't know what to do."

Jane rushed over and hugged her.

"Gin, it will be fine. What did Jake say?"

"I called him, but he's working tonight and very busy. He said he couldn't talk."

"What? That's crazy Ginny, this is very important and he needs to know so you can both decide what you're going to do. You've got to go see him and talk to him. When he knows he'll drop everything to speak to you about this, I'm sure," Jane said.

"I don't know. He really sounded busy. Besides, I'm going to see him tomorrow."

"Ginny, how are you going to sleep tonight? This is crazy, if he loves you, he'll want to know about this!"

"Okay, let me think about this."

Ginny sat on the couch saying nothing. Finally, she stood up and got her coat.

She walked to the subway and took the train uptown to 86th Street. Then she walked west to Madison Avenue. She was about to cross the street when she saw Jake. He was looking at a piece of paper he had pulled out of his pocket. She was about to yell out to him when she saw a short, slim woman with short black hair standing close to him. Maybe she was a co-worker picking up materials or papers for the project he was working on. Maybe she was a neighbor who ran into him on the street to say hello.

Then she watched as the woman leaned in to kiss Jake on his lips as he turned to embrace her. He held the woman for a while, then they both turned and walked hand in hand toward Fifth Avenue.

The traffic light changed five times before Ginny could move.

Chapter Thirty-Two

The sun was brutally hot that day in August on the lawn by the cabin. Connie was in the yard tending to her flowers wearing a wide brimmed straw hat. She pruned her roses with such precision, she could have been a barber.

Cara sat on the deck watching her mother as she sipped her iced tea. Connie had come up for long weekends and was now taking her two-week vacation. The garden looked beautiful this summer. Cara had chosen Marigolds to plant this year. She had planted them with Connie at the corners of the garden to frame the other flowers with their bright orange and yellow flowers.

Cara never felt more at peace. Her relationship with her mother had become one of quiet understanding and accep-tance. When she told her mother that she had feelings for women and that she was unsure how to deal with it, Connie held her and told Cara that she loved her and that everything would be fine, that all she cared about was that she be happy. Cara cried from happiness when Connie said that.

They spent the last weeks of August visiting old friends who lived around the lake, and other friends who rented the same cottages year after year.

Connie invited a colleague for the weekend named Yvonne, who was also a jewelry designer, and her daughter Brie. Cara and Brie hit it off right away. Yvonne and Brie were both tall blondes, standing at 5'9". It created an amusing picture next to the redheads, Connie and Cara, at 5'2" Brie was upbeat, and funny. She had just graduated from Vassar and was starting Columbia Law School in the Fall.

Later that evening Cara asked Brie about her name.

"Brie is an unusual name. Are you named after Bree Daniels, the character played by Jane Fonda in *Klute*? I saw the movie about eight years ago and loved it."

"That was kinda racey for a young girl to see. No, I wasn't named after a high-class prostitute," Brie said laughing. They both were laughing now.

"No, it's worse, my parents were very bohemian when I was born and someone introduced them to Brie cheese and they loved the name," Brie said, rolling her eyes.

"That is great! Most people have such boring names," Cara said.

"I'm just lucky they weren't introduced to Gouda or Camembert cheese!" Brie replied.

They both laughed again.

The four women had a great time that weekend. Brie introduced them to Dirty Scrabble, too, where you can only use lewd or curse words. On their last day Cara and Brie drove to town to shop for food, then came back and took the row boat out. Connie and Yvonne enjoyed their cocktails at happy hour and laughed about their industry gossip. On Sunday, as they all prepared to leave, Cara and Brie exchanged phone numbers to stay in touch in the city in the Fall.

Chapter Thirty-Three

"Ginny, he's calling again, what should I say?" Jane asked as she opened the door to Ginny's bedroom. It was Saturday afternoon and Ginny hadn't gotten out of bed.

"Just tell him I'm still not feeling well please Jane," Ginny said softly.

"Gin, you are going to have to talk to him at some point."

Ginny lay in bed not knowing what to think. Had she really been such a fool?

She didn't get out of bed until five that afternoon. She decided she had to eat something so went to the kitchen and toasted an English muffin. She sat at the small dining table and stared off into space. She went through all the great times she had with Jake. The wonderful dinners, the theater, the museum visits, and their incredible trip to St. Martin. She wondered if she had done something wrong or said something stupid. Had she driven him away?

She was buttering her toasted muffin when the phone rang. She hesitated to pick it up. God, they need to get one of those new answering machines so they can screen the calls.

She walked over to pick it up.

"Ginny, are you ok? Jane told me you don't feel well. Do you need anything?" Jake asked.

"No, I'm fine," Ginny answered flatly.

"Do you want to come over here and I'll take care of you?" he asked.

Ginny wanted to cry. She wanted that more than anything, to be in his arms and have him hold her. She just couldn't bring herself to do it. All she could see over and over again was that woman kissing him and him holding her and kissing her back.

"I can't Jake," Ginny said softly.

"Okay, I'll check in on you in the morning. Feel better sweetheart," Jake said and hung up.

Ginny looked at the phone and wanted to smash it.

An hour later Jane came home. She took one look at Ginny and said, "You have to call Jake back Gin and let him know everything. Or go see him," Jane said.

"Jake called. He wanted me to come by, but I can't now. I'm too confused and upset. I keep thinking I must have done something."

"Ginny stop it! Please don't do this to yourself. This man is dealing with something that is not about you. You however have to let him know you are pregnant with his child and decide what you will do."

"But why would he do this, see someone else behind my back, unless I did something?"

"Oh Gin, because he's got his own issues, that's why. Issues that don't involve you!"

"Okay, I'll see him tomorrow. I can't go today because he'll want me to stay over and I can't do that now."

"That's fine, but know you are always in control of whether you stay with him overnight or not."

"You're right Jane. I'm going to lie down," Ginny went back to her room leaving her food on the dining table.

The following morning Ginny got up around ten. She felt a bit better and stronger even though she hadn't gotten much sleep. She went to the phone and dialed Jake's number. No answer.

Ginny felt angry now. If he cared, he'd be home concerned and waiting to call or for her call. She decided to get dressed and go out for breakfast at her favorite cafe in the neighborhood. She put on makeup to cover the red splotches around her eyes from crying.

When she stepped out she felt good as the hot, August sun heated her up. She walked to a cafe. She saw students already up and out filling the streets. Classes were going to start in about a week on August 30th.

Ginny went in and sat at a small table. She ordered a coffee and stayed for about an hour. As she headed back, she turned to walk toward Washington Square Park instead of going home. She sat on a bench thinking more clearly now. She couldn't keep the child growing in her belly. How in the world would she manage having a child? She couldn't even properly take care of herself, she thought. It was clear that Jake wasn't going to commit to having a child with her right now. She sat in the sun thinking maybe there has to be an explanation for what she saw in front of Jake's apartment and perhaps everything is fine with them. She got up and walked quickly back to her apartment. When she got home, she dialed Jake's number. This time he answered.

"Hi Jake, I'm feeling better. I'm coming up to you," Ginny said.

"Great. I'll see you soon."

Ginny walked west from the subway as she had two days ago and the sick feeling came back to her as she approached the same corner where she saw Jake with the woman.

Riding up the elevator Ginny started to shake. She hated confrontations. She got off the elevator and walked to his apartment. The door was open and he was standing in the doorway as she approached his apartment. He went to hug her, but she limply hugged him back. When inside she went to the black couch and sat down. Jake sat next to her and looked at her.

"Ginny, what's wrong, you look terrible?" he said, taking her hand.

"Jake, I tried to tell you something two days ago, but you wouldn't listen,"

"I was busy with a deadline. I told you," he said, dropping her hand.

"God, you are too much. Jake, when you weren't letting me talk to you, I decided to come up to see you Friday. When I was crossing the street to your apartment building, I saw you kissing another woman outside the entrance to your lobby. So you were busy, but it was not work," Ginny said, with her eyes starting to tear.

Jake stood up.

"Ginny, sweetheart, that was nothing! The woman you saw me with is a very old friend who was in town. We used to date many years ago and so we kissed, so what? I walked her to the bus stop and then I went back upstairs to work. You can't seriously think it's something else? Come on!" Jake said, putting on the charm.

"Jake, you really expect me to believe that?" Ginny said, staring at him.

Now he started to get angry.

"Honestly, I'm shocked with what I'm hearing. You're un-believable!" Jake said, starting to shout. He was pacing back and forth across the living room.

"First off, my time is my time Ginny, not yours to question. Just because you couldn't wait to tell me something, you had to run up here and sneak around and check up on me!" he shouted, then continued, "How dare you! I've been nothing but good to you Ginny. I dote on you showing you the best nights out you've ever had! I even took you on a wonderful vacation and now you treat me like this?"

Ginny was sobbing now.

"Jake, I'm pregnant," she choked out.

"Oh Jesus!" Jake yelled and raised his arms up.

This was not what Ginny expected. She wanted him to hold her, soothe her and make her fears go away. Instead, she felt awful. She had never heard him raise his voice to her before. When Cara and she were children, he was always so patient and kind. Who was this man in front of her?

"What happened to your birth control? You have to take care of it. Do you know where to go? I'll pay for it of course. Just tell me when," Jake said, raising his voice.

Ginny looked at him shocked. She couldn't say anything. She was shaking uncontrollably. She told herself to calm down. It would be no good to break down in front of him. All she knew is that she had to get out of there. She slowly stood up and walked to his front door.

"Now, you're leaving? We need to discuss when you will look into taking care of this."

She opened the door and walked out.

Chapter Thirty-Four

The wooden box smashed against the wall so hard that it made a large dent. Jake was furious. He was so wrong about Ginny. He thought because she was so young that he could help her become the woman he always wanted and needed. He had shown her what it was like to have the finer things in life, how to live well, and now she treated him like this? He trusted her, but obviously she didn't trust him. Having a family was not what he needed or wanted now, especially with a woman who snuck around spying on him. She turned out to be like so many of the other women he had known who were not only demanding, but untrustworthy. He remembered Amanda who, after taking her away on a luxurious trip, was angry that he went out with a friend for drinks the night they returned.

He started to think, did Ginny purposefully get herself pregnant in order for him to marry her or worse try to get money from him? What if she decided to keep the child, what then? Twenty-one years of child support, that's what, he told himself. He started to panic. He had to make sure she would take care of this, but how? He couldn't drag her in to get an abortion. You can't force someone to get one.

He was pacing the room. Then he had an idea. He dialed a florist. He ordered three dozen white roses to send to Ginny with a note. "My Ginny, Please forgive me, I was a fool. I love you! Jake." He hung up pleased with himself.

He'd wait till this evening and then call her.

At six o'clock, Jake dialed Ginny's phone number. No answer. At six thirty, no answer. He decided to go to dinner at the small French restaurant around the corner. After two glasses of wine, he felt himself starting to calm down. He needed to think. He kept thinking of the possibility of Ginny going ahead with the pregnancy. He would try calling her again when he got home. As he walked home, he started to feel bad. He really should not have yelled at Ginny. She was, after all, very young and immature. Her spying on him was something he'll talk to her more about and he would set her straight on that. But before that, he would make sure that she would want and desire him as she had before. He needed to ensure that she would do what was needed to do.

He entered his apartment, poured himself a vodka, and settled down on his couch with the phone on his lap ready to dial. Jake planned to ask Ginny to please come back to his place so he could properly hold her and tell her everything would be alright. He rehearsed what he would say. "Sweetheart, you know how much I care for you, I was having such a bad day with all these deadlines. Please come up to see me, or I can come to you. Please forgive me," he'd say. Then he thought he would take her to a fine restaurant this coming week before school started, maybe Wednesday night. That would make her happy. He would tell her everything would be fine with them and when the time is right, he would tell everyone about their relationship and they could move forward with plans for the future. He would explain how right now was not the right time to start a family, but in a couple of years, it would be. He'd tell her he didn't realize how much she meant to him until they had this first argument, that he realized that she is so special to him and he didn't want to lose her. He smiled, feeling confident.

He dialed Ginny's number again.

No answer.

Chapter Thirty-Five

"Hi Ginny! No hon, Cara's not home now. She's parking the car. We just got home from Lake George. Can she call you back later?" Connie asked.

"Of course, thank you," Ginny said.

"Ginny, how are you? Sorry I missed seeing you this summer. Maybe you can come to Lake George this Fall? It's so beautiful there when the leaves are turning. You must come!"

"Thank you so much, I'll try."

"I'll tell Cara you called," Connie said.

Ginny hung up, thinking what in the world would she tell Cara? The truth she thought. The truth about everything. She had been seeing Jake for almost a year now. What would Cara think of her? What would Connie think of her? She was too old to try to pass it off that she was so innocent in this relationship. She knew something should be said to Cara and Jake's sister, Connie, but it was his responsibility to do that, right? She now started to dread Cara calling her back.

Jane came home just after Ginny hung up from speaking to Connie. She was holding an enormous bouquet of white roses with two hands.

"These were sitting outside our door. I guess they didn't think anyone was home," Jane said.

Ginny took the three dozen white roses inside and read the note from Jake. Her hand went to her mouth as she started to cry.

Jane read the note. "Come on, we are going out. You need to clear your head. Besides, you look like you should eat something."

Ginny nodded and the two of them went out to the Caliente Cab Company, the Mexican restaurant in the Village. As they entered, they ran into a couple of Jane's classmates. They all sat down together and ordered guacamole and a pitcher of margaritas.

Ginny picked at the guacamole, but didn't fill her glass with the margarita. Jane looked at Ginny as if to ask her if she wanted to drink. Ginny shook her head. One of Jane's friends was a guy who had a good sense of humor, who made the evening lively. Jane's other friends welcomed Ginny in the conversation and she started to feel good. She tried to picture Jake sitting here with a bunch of twenty-year olds hanging out, talking about their classes, relationships etc. Forget it. He would stick out like a sore thumb and it would be so awkward. She was enjoying this evening. These were her peers and where she fit in. She didn't fit into Jake's world. What even was his world? All he seemed to do was work. As she sat there, she started to ask herself why exactly did she love Jake?

She ordered quesadillas, and halfway through eating them, she reached for the pitcher of margaritas and poured herself a glass, then another. She knew then what she had to do.

Chapter Thirty-Six

Cara tried to return Ginny's call a few times that night. Her guess was that Ginny wanted to get together before school started again for their senior year. Cara was feeling good. She had worked on her portfolio and thought it looked good. She would continue to add to it and she would be ready to start interviewing for jobs after the holidays she thought. She told herself she would ask Jake about illustrator openings at Benton & Bowles.

The following day Cara was getting ready to do her laundry and she was cleaning out her jean pockets, when she found the paper with Brie's phone number. She smiled and thought she must give her a call. She really enjoyed meeting her. Was it too soon to call her? They were all just together. She told herself that was ridiculous. She dialed her number.

"Hello?"

"Hi Brie, this is Cara. It was so nice to meet you this past week. I know we both just got back, but I was wondering if you'd like to get together some time?"

"Cara! I'm so glad you called! I'd love to get together. I'm kinda busy this week...but wait, I'm getting together with my girlfriend and a couple of other friends around noon today for a picnic lunch in Central Park. Do you want to join us? It should be a lot of fun," Brie said.

"Oh, I'd love to! I'll make a pasta salad that we can all share."

"Wonderful, we will be on the lawn across from Tavern on the Green. You won't miss us. We'll be the loud ones!"

Cara smiled, Brie was always upbeat and it was infectious. It will be fun to meet her friends...and her girlfriend. Why did she say "her girlfriend"? Wouldn't her friend who's a girl just be part of her friends? Anyway, it's going to be fun and she'll meet new interesting people.

She packed the pasta salad in the Tupperware container and took the subway downtown. As she entered the park, she saw a group of four people sitting on blankets opening up coolers and bags of food to put out. Brie saw her and waved her over. She walked faster to them and introduced herself and added her dish to the sharing pile in the center of the blankets. Brie introduced her friends. There was Javier, Walt and Maria.

Javier and Walt knew Brie from childhood and Maria went to college with her. Maria must be the girlfriend. Maria was a short, fair-haired girl with piercing green eyes. She also had a warm and bubbly personality. Maria was already working at Doubleday as an assistant to a book editor.

Javier was one of Brie's oldest friends. He had known Brie when they were both in elementary school in the Bronx. He had a good sense of humor and like Brie, pulled you into the fun. He was working as a waiter while he went on acting auditions. Cara saw him put his arm around Walt who was also an aspiring actor. Walt had said something funny about an audition Javier had and Javier playfully pushed him, then pulled him back in to kiss his cheek.

She then looked at Brie and Maria who were sitting close together. Cara noticed they sometimes put their hand on each other's knee or touched the hand of the other. It was subtle, but she could feel the affection they had for each other. She was also seeing what she wished she would have one day. Cara admired that they were so free to express their love for each other. She had seen gay classmates at Music and Art, but they were not as open as this. She had even suspected Matt from high school of being gay, but it was never discussed. It was also refreshing to see everyone comfortable with themselves.

The conversation was lively, discussing president Carter and the possible change in next year's election. They all pointed out President Carter's good points and the fear of having Reagan in the White House. They spoke about Earth Day last April and if anything would be done to save our planet. Then they all spoke of jobs they were starting or the colleges they were attending for graduate school. Brie was excited about starting her med school courses at Columbia and thought she would specialize in pediatrics. Cara was impressed with everyone. They were all just a year older than she was, but they seemed more, starting new chapters in their lives.

As it got later in the afternoon, people started to clean up. Cara helped Brie and Maria pack the last few things and they walked out of the park together. She noticed Brie and Maria holding hands.

"Brie, do you live close by?" Cara asked.

"Maria and I have a small one bedroom on 84th Street in a brownstone. We'll have you over for dinner soon," Brie said.

"That would be lovely. I'd like that. Great to meet you Maria. I'm going to head west to the subway. I'll see you again soon," Cara said as they all hugged and headed in different directions.

Cara had such a good time that day. She felt comfortable around Brie and her friends because they were comfortable with themselves. They were completely open about their thoughts and feelings about different issues, but also completely free and at ease with who they were. Just being around all them made her feel good.

Chapter Thirty-Seven

The phone rang, Jane was in her own bedroom, so Ginny went to pick it up.

"Sweetheart, I've been trying to reach you since yesterday," Jake said.

He continued, "I'm so sorry about yesterday, I guess I was in shock and handled it really badly. Did you get the flowers?" He asked.

"Yes Jake, thank you. Listen, I really don't want to talk right now. I actually feel it's better that we not see each other for a while. I need to clear my head," Ginny said.

"Ginny, I need to see you. I'll come down to you after work today, please,?' he pleaded.

"All right, but Jane will be here. We can meet somewhere else nearby, I guess," Ginny said.

"Great! I'll make a reservation somewhere wonderful."

"Jake, no don't! I am just meeting you quickly because it's something you want to do. We can get a coffee somewhere."

Ginny hung up feeling nothing. She never knew she could feel so dead inside.

After work he picked her up in front of her building and they walked to a coffee shop. She sensed that he was very anxious. Even when he sat, he couldn't sit still.

"Ginny, you know how much I care about you. Please let's discuss this like two adults and try to figure out what needs to be done. You know, this is not the time for either of us to be starting a family. You still have a whole year left of college and then you have your career that you want to move forward with. My career keeps me so busy and it requires a lot of travel. One day Ginny, one day we will both be ready for this and it will be wonderful. Just not now, you understand, don't you?"

"I'm curious, what if I said I want to keep the baby?" she asked.

"Ginny, no! You can't do that. It would destroy both of us. Please Ginny."

Seeing the panic in his face brought her a kind of pleasure knowing she had a certain power.

"So, you don't want to be a father?" she asked, knowing it would make him squirm.

"God, Ginny not now! Please think about this! Can you imagine us as parents now? Come on!" His voice was raised and people in the coffee shop turned to look at them.

Ginny looked at him and realized that he was right, that she also could not imagine them as parents now. The problem was that she couldn't imagine them as parents in the future either. She was in love with this man and couldn't understand why he was acting like this. Jake didn't seem like a sophisticated man full of confidence and full of life. In this coffee shop he seemed like an insecure little boy who was scared that things would not go the way he wanted, that his much younger pregnant girlfriend would ruin the life he imagined for himself. He didn't even seem to consider her feelings through this. He wanted her to choose what was convenient for him.

She started to feel nauseous and told Jake she didn't feel well and needed to get home.

Jake was panicking. He couldn't let her go.

"Ginny, you need to take care of this," Jake said, shouting not caring if people were staring at him.

"Jake, relax. I'll do what I need to do," Ginny said as she stood up and started to walk toward the exit door.

Jake threw money on the table for their two coffees and followed her out of the coffee shop.

"Ginny, I love you," Jake said, taking her hand.

"Jake. I have to go." Ginny said and pulled her hand away and turned walking east to her apartment. She had finally heard the words she wanted to hear for so long and now they meant nothing.

Jake stood in the street watching Ginny's back as she walked away.

The following morning, she called the school health office. She explained her situation and they gave her the phone number and address of a clinic. She called the clinic and they told her they were only open during weekdays, and that she could schedule her abortion for the following week. The fee for the abortion was $400. That would wipe out her entire savings, but she didn't care. She didn't want to ask Jake for anything now. Her schedule was light on Fridays so if she had to miss classes, it would only be two. She scheduled her appointment at the clinic that following Friday.

Chapter Thirty-Eight

Jake hated himself for losing control as he did. He could feel his blood pressure rising. Why was Ginny doing this? This was not the little shy girl he knew. She had turned into a bitch just like the rest of them, demanding and conniving. He walked uptown thinking he would grab a cab halfway home. He kept walking and thinking. What was he going to do? He could deny the baby was his. No one knew he was seeing her. Not Cara or Connie, no one. It was a good thing he didn't let anyone know. There was Jane of course, but who would believe a roommate of a silly twenty-year old.

This is why he liked Iris. She had absolutely no demands on him whatsoever. He needed to change dates, fine. He wanted to see her at the last minute because he had a need, no problem. Iris was only five years younger than he so he knew she wasn't looking to start a family. He liked younger women, but Iris knew his sexual tastes and that came with experience younger women just didn't have. Sure, he liked teaching Ginny, but after a while it got tiring. He wanted someone with whom he didn't have to take charge, someone who would make suggestions of where to go and what to do because they've experienced it or they've read up on what's going on. Yes, Iris was more suited to him. Besides, even if he had his outside dalliances and if she suspected, she never said anything or complained. Iris also had her own life. She had her yoga that she practiced and she also taught yoga classes at the yoga center downtown. She wasn't sitting around waiting for him. That being said, when he needed her, she was available. He liked that.

He'd have to make sure Ginny took care of this, he kept telling himself. He planned to call her every day to find out what she planned to do. Then he thought, maybe he could pay her to do it. He could pay her last year's tuition. Promise to marry her next year. Anything to get her to not have a child that would be a burden to him for the next twenty-one years.

He kept thinking as he walked and he soon realized that he was on 68th Street and Fifth Avenue. He might as well walk the rest of the way.

Chapter Thirty-Nine

Cara was home preparing her books for her first class the next day. She was excited to start her final year. She decided she definitely wanted to pursue illustration in some form whether it be books or in advertising. Her first love was still to illustrate children's books, but that was hard to break into, so she would start anywhere to gain experience.

She had left a message for her Uncle Jake at work to ask his opinion, but he hadn't returned her call. She even tried him at home, but he always seemed to be out.

She was sorting things when she realized that she also hadn't reached Ginny. It had been a couple of days and she knew Ginny was starting school too tomorrow and must be busy. She dialed her number.

"Hi Ginny! Sorry I missed your call. I was actually going to call you to see if you wanted to get together before we start classes for the Fall. I can't believe we are in our last year!"

"I know. Sure, I'd love to see you," Ginny said. She couldn't hide her voice sounding down.

"Ginny, I know you, you sound funny, is anything wrong?"

"It's difficult to explain over the phone. Let's talk when we get together."

"So, let's see each other tomorrow. Do you want me to come by you?"

"I think Jane will be home. Let's meet in Washington Square Park. Call me before you leave and we'll pick a spot," Ginny said.

Cara hung up puzzled. Ginny sounded awful. Maybe it had something to do with her parents, or maybe Sara, with whom she had never gotten along. Ginny had been the happiest she had seen her in years lately, almost giddy at times. She knew she was in love with that guy she was seeing. What was his name again, she thought, then she remembered, Gene. Maybe it had something to do with Gene?

The phone rang and it was Jake returning her call from work.

"Hey, how's my favorite niece? What can I do for you?" Jake asked cheerfully.

"Hi Uncle Jake, I've worked all summer on my portfolio and I was wondering when entry level positions for illustrators at Benton and Bowles will be posted? I've decided I want to get into illustration for my career," Cara said.

"Look at you, all ready to go and start working! The entry positions won't be posted for a while. Probably in the Spring next year, right before you graduate, you should apply. I'll keep an eye out for postings, I promise."

"Thanks Uncle Jake. I hope you come by for dinner soon or just come by to say hi. We missed you this summer."

"I know kiddo, I've been so busy, but I'll stop by soon. How's Connie?"

"She's fine, doing better, but would love to see you."

"Give her a hug and kiss from me. I'll see you soon."

Cara hung up feeling happy. She would pursue publishers to see if any books coming out could use her talent, but she could count on Jake getting her into advertising, she told herself. She opened her portfolio to add the work she had done the last couple of days. She planned to edit her book depending on the interviews she would go on. The publishing houses would see more illustrations of animals, figure drawings and landscapes. For advertising companies, she would show her more graphic work using logos and themes. She would include her book cover illustrations in both categories. She continued to move her art pieces around and edit for the rest of the day.

Chapter Forty

The following morning Ginny's phone rang early and it was Cara saying she'd come down around eleven thirty. She would pick up sandwiches and they could have lunch while they sat in the park. They planned to meet under the arch in Washington Square. Ginny started to shake. She was dreading seeing Cara not knowing what she would say.

At eleven fifteen Ginny walked to the park and saw Cara was already there.

"I made good time getting down here. Hey, that bench is free over there, let's grab it," Cara said.

They both sat on the bench as Cara opened the paper bag and handed Ginny her turkey sandwich.

"Are you looking forward to this year? I think it will be exciting. I can't wait to start looking for jobs too!" Cara said smiling.

Ginny did not smile back.

"Now tell me, what's going on Ginny? I don't remember you looking so depressed. Is it Gene?

"Who's Gene?" Ginny asked.

"Umm...your boyfriend, remember?" Cara said, with a chuckle.

"Cara, I don't know how to tell you. I've been seeing some-one for about a year now. It's been amazing and I've been wanting to talk to you more about it, but something has happened and I'm scared. I know what I have to do, but I feel sick about it," Ginny said.

"I'm trying to follow you. Did Gene do something?"

"There's no Gene, Cara."

"So...who is this person? I don't understand."

"It's Jake Cara. I've been seeing Jake. I didn't know how to tell you," Ginny said, looking down.

"Wait, what? My Uncle Jake!" Cara said, turning to face Ginny.

Ginny nodded.

"When, when did this start?"

"Last November."

"I'm sorry Ginny, but I'm...I don't know what to say," Cara said.

"You don't have to say anything. I'm so sorry I didn't tell you. I kept waiting for him to say something to you." Ginny replied.

"I just realized you were together at Mel's funeral. You both worked hard at concealing this, didn't you? Were you with Jake on your vacation too?" Cara asked, sounding angry now.

"Yes. I'm so sorry Cara. I wanted to tell you, but right now I really need you as my friend. Something has happened and it seems that Jake and I will not be together anymore."

"What's happening Ginny?" Cara asked very quietly.

"I'm pregnant Cara," Ginny said, looking down.

Cara stared at her in disbelief. Then she turned to look away and shook her head.

"Oh Jesus! Well...what are you both going to do? Are there marriage plans?" Cara said, turning back to Ginny.

"No, I told you we may not be together anymore. He has made it clear that he wants me to get an abortion. I have an

appointment next Friday. I'm scared Cara and I really wanted to talk to you about this. He hasn't been very supportive
about this whole situation."

"Ginny, you are speaking to me about my beloved uncle. I
will need to speak to him about this. I have to ask you, what
birth control were you using?"

"Diaphragm, but it failed. Cara, he was my first. I know that
doesn't mean anything to you, but it did to me. I loved him,
and maybe I guess I still do. Please don't speak to him. He'll
just get angrier at me," Ginny said, anxiously.

Cara was silent. She calmed down and was softening. Ginny
was starting to cry. Beautiful Ginny now looked so scared.

"He'll get more angry at you? So, tell me, is he taking you for
the procedure next Friday?" Cara asked.

"I don't know, I didn't ask. He's pretty angry now."

"He's angry? Is he blaming you for getting pregnant?"

"I don't know, maybe," Ginny said softly.

Cara's head was spinning. Jake? What the hell was he doing
seducing Ginny? If he truly loved her, why didn't he tell her
or Connie? Her stomach started to turn over and she felt sick
about all she was hearing. She looked again at Ginny who
looked so desperate sitting there crying. Jake did this to her

Ginny, whom she loved so much. How could he abandon her like this?

"I'll go with you next Friday, just tell me the time and place."

Chapter Forty-One

Jake threw himself into his work. He tried not to think about Ginny, or the "problem". At work he spoke to Stewart, who was his new single buddy. Stewart was around thirty years old, had left a relationship about a year ago and was now dating quite a bit. He and Jake would often go for a drink after work. Tonight, there was a late meeting and they both agreed they needed to wind down, so they went to a local bar, had some beers and ate bar food. Stewart spoke of his date last weekend, and how the girl insisted on splitting the tab.

"As far as I'm concerned, when a woman does that, she's telling you that she is not interested. She is basically saying that she doesn't want to be beholden to you for anything. She's independent and doesn't need you to take care of her. Her being independent is fine, but there are dating norms and if you don't want to accept that, then you're telling the guy that you're not interested. Do you agree?" Stewart asked.

"I don't know. I've met some women who feel more comfortable paying their own way, even if they are in a relationship with you. I don't care for that either, because other aspects of their personality come along with that. Those women tend to want everything to be shared, like cooking and cleaning up, and they force their opinions on every subject. I prefer a woman who's old fashioned and lets me take charge. I'm happy to take care of a woman, but I guess I like being the man in control. There are, however, some situations you can't control." Jake said.

"Like what?" Stewart asked.

"Like a woman getting herself pregnant."

"Oh shit, Jake, did that happen to you before."

"Not before, now. I don't know what she's going to do, but she better do the right thing. That is what I have no control over and it's killing me. You know if she has this child, my life is going to be hell with child support payments and I may have to give her some settlement," Jake said.

"I have to ask, do you love her? Is there a possibility of marriage?" Stewart asked.

"You know, I thought so at one point, but I feel she was manipulative in how she dealt with this. I mean, she was supposed to be on birth control. Honestly Stewart, I think I'm also getting bored with her. She looks to me to introduce her to everything and nods in agreement with every opinion I have. Come on, when is she going to have her own thoughts? She's a child in so many ways."

"But then, the woman with a lot of thoughts, opinions and independence would drive you crazy too, no?" Stewart asked.

"Well, ya know what they say, 'can't live with them, can't live without them', right?" Jake replied, taking a big gulp from his beer.

He asked Stewart if he wanted to get together on Saturday. He really didn't feel like seeing Ginny this weekend.

Stewart said he'd have to let him know because he might have a date. He was waiting to hear back from a girl.

Jake didn't say anything, but thought Stewart was a fool waiting for the woman to decide. He should move on. He now saw Stewart as being weak.

He went home and switched Iris to Saturday. He wasn't going to wait for Stewart either. Friday night he'd plan to work late. He didn't bother calling Ginny to let her know. He now decided he would not call her until she took care of the "problem".

Chapter Forty-Two

Cara stayed with Ginny in the park until dusk, then walked Ginny to her apartment, gave her a long hug and told her she would see her next Friday.

Cara would have to miss a class that day to take Ginny to the clinic, but she would talk to the teacher about getting the class material early.

After dropping Ginny off, her mind was racing as she walked to the subway. Ginny asked that she not confront Jake, so right now she would respect that. She felt strange telling her mother about this because she would want to hear Jake's side. Jake's side she thought, what was that anyway? Jake is forty-six years old and Ginny is twenty. Ginny was not a femme fatale seducing Jake. Cara also knew Jake with women and his need to conquer. Why Ginny, Jesus, Jake!

If Jake really cared for Ginny, why didn't he just tell her or Connie? Because Jake knew it wasn't right, that he was playing with Ginny, that it wasn't a serious relationship. Was that why he wasn't coming around much, or even calling for that matter?

As she rode the subway uptown, she realized she would have a hard time seeing Jake now. Cara did not have a poker face and he'd know immediately something wasn't right the minute he saw her. She would have to avoid him. The more she thought about Jake with Ginny, the more she began to hate him. She hated him not only for seducing her best friend, but for her own relationship with him now being jeopardized. She adored her Uncle Jake, now this. How could he do this?

When Cara got home, she and Connie ate dinner together, and as they did Cara watched her mother. Connie, who was so tough most of the time, would be crushed to learn what her little brother, the brother she adored, had done. Then she wondered if Connie would blame Ginny for what happened. Would she see Ginny as the seductress who got herself pregnant for financial gain? Cara thought of the photos she saw in the country house of Jake and Connie's childhood together. Her mother spoke of the fun times as children and the closeness they had. Connie wanted to protect Jake from the teasing he got as a child and saw how cruel children can be. Has that feeling of being cast out and bullied stayed with

Jake? Now that he can get any woman he wants, he makes sure to push them away, the way they all rejected him before?

She wanted to feel sorry for him. The self-loathing he must feel. He is still that fat little boy of fifteen. Then she remembered the pain in Ginny's face telling her what was happening. Ginny clearly loved Jake and probably still does, she thought. This will affect forever how she sees her uncle. She looked down at her left wrist and saw the gold bracelet Jake gave her at her high school graduation lunch. She opened the clasp and took it off.

Chapter Forty-Three

Classes began that Thursday, and Jane left early for her eight thirty class. Ginny had a class at ten o'clock and she was still in bed. She hadn't slept all night and was exhausted. So she misses her first class, so what, she told herself. She also had a two o'clock class. She slept until one thirty in the afternoon and barely made it. When she got to her class, she didn't hear what the professor was saying. She only heard the muted trombone sounds of adults speaking as in the Peanuts animated cartoons. Just a sound droning away in her ears, not making sense.

She walked out of the classroom and she remembered saying hello to some fellow classmates, but couldn't remember what was said. She was starting to get a headache. She got home at four thirty after her class and went to bed. At six thirty she got up and realized she hadn't eaten all day. Jane came out of her room very cheerful and asked how her first day of classes were. One look at Ginny and she asked what was wrong. Ginny was nibbling on some crackers in the kitchen and said she thought she was coming down with something.

The following morning it was the same thing, she just couldn't get up and she missed her two Friday classes. Jane told her to go to see the school nurse and maybe they could give her something. She said she'd rest over the weekend and go Tuesday if she was still sick. Luckily it was Labor Day weekend and had Monday off, she thought.

She was so upset with Jake, but she wanted to hear from him. His not calling made her feel worse, as though he was angry at her. Should she just call him and tell him she was going to take care of the "problem"? She wanted *him* to call. She wanted *him* to say "whatever you want to do, I'm supporting you. I am here for you." Instead, silence. He must have known that she would not jeopardize her future or his for that matter, Ginny thought. What she wanted from him, he was incapable of giving.

Jake didn't call over Labor Day weekend and Ginny sank deeper into a depression. She kept running the conversation she had with Jake at his apartment over and over again. Ginny couldn't shut her thoughts down. Jane tried to get her out of the house, but she refused. On Tuesday Jane told her she should speak to the nurse at school, that maybe the school had a counselor to speak to. Ginny didn't call the school nurse or go to classes.

On late Tuesday afternoon, Jane found Cara's number on Ginny's Rolodex and called. She didn't get an answer all day until around four. Finally, Cara answered.

"Cara, this is Jane, Ginny's roommate. I'm very concerned about Ginny. She hasn't been going to classes and she's just been in bed for days."

Cara said she would come down right away. Cara was now really worried. She had never seen Ginny as such a fragile person before, but she had also never been in this kind of situation before. Cara left a note for her mother telling her she was seeing a friend for dinner and left.

On the way downtown Cara was scared for Ginny. Her depression seemed to be consuming her. With everything that went on with Ginny's parents and with her father's abandonment, she had always felt Ginny could deal with problems. Then Cara realized that Ginny handled family issues in the past by coming downstairs to her apartment and visiting Cara, Connie and Mel and sometimes Jake when she was a child. Cara's family was her escape. She had no escape now because one of Cara's family had caused the problem and had abandoned her.

Chapter Forty-Four

Iris was due any minute now and he had made an eight o' clock dinner reservation at The Palm restaurant in midtown Manhattan. Jake laid out on his bed what he was going to wear. He placed his favorite dark gray suit, white shirt and navy foulard tie on the bedspread looking as if a ghost was wearing them.

It was Saturday night, normally Ginny's night. He told himself it was her fault that they are not together tonight. Her fault for not being more careful. Her fault for not dealing with this "problem" immediately.

When he was finally dressed, he looked himself up and down in the mirror and made some adjustments on his lapel and sleeves, then combed his hair back. When he was satisfied, he went into the living room and poured himself a scotch and soda.

When Iris finally arrived, she was wearing a tight black dress and heels. With her short black hair and red lipstick, she looked quite the vixen. Jake liked that dress. She was dressed for sex, and that was just fine.

At The Palm, Iris ordered the salmon and Jake ordered the prime rib. He then ordered two vodka martinis for them. He listened to Iris talking about the Yoga classes she was teaching. Then she said something about rearranging the garden at her mother's home in Port Washington. Jake nodded and said some "reallys" and "greats", but didn't hear what she was saying.

At one point Iris took Jake's hand and said, "you poor thing, you must be working so hard."

Jake just nodded, smiled and ordered two more martinis. Iris put her hand up to gesture that she didn't want another. Jake told the waiter to bring two anyway, and as the waiter walked away, he told her he'd have the other martini too. Iris sighed, but didn't say anything. She looked at Jake and he seemed lost in thought and pensive. Was something going wrong at work? An account perhaps?

He ordered the carrot cake for dessert to share. Iris tried to start a conversation about how real estate prices were rising so quickly that she wasn't sure it could last. Jake nodded in agreement, then took a sip of his drink. The carrot cake arrived looking like a slice off a thirty-inch cake. They took turns taking bites. Iris stopped after three forkfuls and Jake proceeded to polish it off between sips of the third martini. Iris started to ask what was going on, but knew better. He would tell her when he was ready.

They took a cab back to his apartment and once inside, Jake grabbed Iris in the living room and started to pull off her dress. She turned to face him and his face looked crazed. She told him to take it easy, that she needed to zip it off. She unzipped her dress and dropped it to the floor. Jake then looked her over and ordered her to completely undress. She complied. Jake rapidly removed his clothing and threw them wherever they would land. He reached for Iris and pulled her down onto the rug and climbed on top of her, penetrating her while holding her arms pinned down over her head, restraining her. The sex was angry, driven, and rough. He was like a starving animal that finally was consuming his prey. With each thrust he was taking a bigger bite, devouring her body.

Afterward they both lay on the floor exhausted. Iris felt bruised and her body ached, but she took her tiny hand and reached to find his. When found, she held his hand tightly.

Chapter Forty-Five

Jane opened the door for Cara. Ginny was sitting at the dining table trying to eat the soup that Jane had prepared for her.

Cara gave Ginny a hug, then pulled a chair closer to her. Ginny had visibly lost weight. Jane stood by watching, worried.

"Ginny, I love you and I'm concerned. You are suffering and you need to talk to someone about what's going on. Please let me help you get help. I'll get the phone number of the health office at NYU and I'll make an appointment for you to speak to a counselor. I'll schedule it so I can go with you. Have you attended any classes?" Cara asked.

Ginny held up one finger.

"Ok, well, the health office can let the professors know you've been ill. No worries. But let's deal with what's going on right now. You must eat and get your strength up," Cara said, wanting to curse out Jake and tell her to forget him, but she decided that might make matters worse.

Jane looked at Cara and motioned that she was going to her room to give them time alone.

"You are such a good person who deserves the best and to be treated well. No person should have this affect on you Ginny," Cara said, taking Ginny's hand.

"Cara, I'm so sorry to be causing you such concern. I realized that even though I know what I need to do I still feel sick about it. There is a life growing inside of me. I've always been pro-choice and still am, but now it's me facing it. It's a decision I never thought I would have to face. You know, if I were older and was living on my own independently and could afford it, I'd go ahead and have this child. I'd try to make the best life for this little person who was from Jake and me," Ginny said.

Hearing Jake's name coming out of Ginny's mouth made Cara want to smash something.

"You don't know how you would feel if this were happening when you had a career and had to face paying a fortune for child care or taking years off to raise a child. It is very difficult. Don't go down a path you really don't know. Right now, you have to eat and get stronger."

Cara went into the kitchen to see what she could make for them to eat. In the cabinet to the left of the stove she found some penne pasta. She couldn't find any sauce anywhere. She opened the refrigerator and found three sad looking tomatoes and some olives in a jar. She cut up the tomatoes and olives and put them in a pan with olive oil she found on the counter. When the pasta was ready, she heated the pan until the tomatoes were soft, then poured the olives and tomatoes onto the cooked penne and mixed them up.

She served Ginny a large portion and gave herself a small one. She smiled when Ginny asked for some salt and pepper to season the pasta as she had forgotten to do so. She was happy to see Ginny eating and that she actually finished her plate.

"Thank you, Cara. I love you for being here," Ginny said.

"I love you too."

The next morning Cara took the phone into her bedroom to call the NYU health office. Connie hadn't left yet, and Cara didn't want her to overhear her conversation. The person who answered the phone sounded gruff. Cara explained that she was a friend of a student that needed to speak to a counselor right away. The woman asked to speak to the student. Cara said that wasn't possible right now and that the situation was serious. The woman asked if it was an emergency because if so, she should call 911. Frustrated, Cara said that she thought her friend just might need some medication to help her through this difficult time. Finally, the woman said that an appointment was available the following day which was Wednesday at 9 am.

Cara called Ginny to tell her about the appointment and that she would pick her up at her apartment the following morning at 8:30 to take her there.

Cara arrived at Ginny's that morning and they both walked to the health office. Ginny did seem stronger, and told Cara that she finally got some sleep the night before.

They entered the office and there was a student already waiting, quietly coughing. Ginny went to the front desk to check in. After fifteen minutes a nurse came out and called Ginny's name. Both Ginny and Cara stood up.

"Only Ginny," The nurse said.

"Please, I want my friend with me," Ginny said.

"Unfortunately, those are the rules."

Cara sat down quietly mumbling a curse word as Ginny followed the nurse to a back room.

After a half hour Ginny came out holding a piece of paper. She walked over to the counter to check out.

She showed Cara the prescription for Fluoxetine.

"The doctor said this should help me feel better. He also said that he would contact my professors to let them know I had been ill and that I should be able to make up my classes," Ginny said smiling.

Cara went with Ginny to the pharmacist to fill her prescription and waited with her until it was filled.

When outside Cara gave Ginny a hug and told her she'd pick her up Friday to take her to the clinic. Then Cara walked west, heading to the subway.

Chapter Forty-Six

"Hey Cara, it's Brie, I wanted to reach out because Maria and I are throwing a little party this Saturday night. Can you come?"

"Oh that sounds great! Yes I'll be there! Let me know what I can bring," Cara answered.

"Just yourself, we have everything covered. They'll be some fun people there. Walt and Javier, who you met in the park, are coming too."

Cara hung up feeling so good. This was exactly what she needed.

Cara had some assignments due Friday that she decided to turn in on Thursday. She planned to spend all day Friday with Ginny. The appointment at the clinic was at ten in the morning. Cara called Friday morning before heading downtown, and Ginny did not sound good. When Cara arrived, she thought Ginny looked very tired.

"I haven't slept and my stomach is a mess. I think it's this medication. I'm also scared of this procedure Cara," Ginny said.

"I'll be there for you, don't worry. Do mention you are taking Fluoxetine at the clinic."

When they arrived at the clinic on West 15th Street, Ginny walked to the check-in counter, wrote a check for $400 then sat down.

There were other women there already, some with men and some with a female friend to help them home. All were waiting to get examined, get advice on care during their pregnancy, or to end their pregnancy. Ginny looked at the two pregnant women in the room. They had men with them. She could see how happy they were. She imagined that they would go on to have happy home lives with beautiful children. Then she looked at the women who sat with friends like Cara. Friends who were there to support their friend at a time of need with their "problem". Ginny could feel herself starting to cry. Cara put her arm around her.

"Why in the world do they put pregnant women in the same waiting room as women having a procedure? Are they doing this to test whether you still want to go through with it, Jesus," Cara whispered not too softly. A woman with a friend across from them looked at Cara, smiled and nodded.

"Ginny Harris?" A friendly looking nurse assistant called out.

Ginny raised her hand, hugged Cara and disappeared into the hallway leading to the exam rooms.

Cara sat looking around the room wondering how many abortions were being done that day. How many Ginnys were here? Women that either had their birth control fail, were raped, were just not careful enough, or simply did not want to be mothers. They all had to face this awful decision and no matter how certain these women were with that decision, it was agonizing.

After an hour and a half, the same nurse assistant came to Cara and asked her to follow her. She took Cara to a room where Ginny was lying on a hospital bed. Ginny was groggy, but looked up and smiled at her when she saw her friend. Cara took a seat next to the bed and touched Ginny's shoulder.

"Hey, how are you doing?" Cara asked.

Ginny just nodded and closed her eyes, seeming to drift off.

After around twenty minutes the doctor came in smiling. She seemed almost cheerful, with her short blonde hair and hoop earrings. Cara wondered how much training in smiling these doctors had to do.

"Well Miss Harris, you are going to be fine. You'll need to use these for about a week," the doctor said, showing Ginny some packaged Kotex. "Take Tylenol, not aspirin if you feel pain or discomfort."

Ginny nodded.

"Should she continue with Fluoxetine?" Cara asked.

"Fluoxetine? You didn't mention you were taking that," the doctor said, looking at Ginny and then Cara.

Cara looked at Ginny and said, "you never told the doctor?"

"Why are you taking that? Who prescribed it?" The doctor asked.

"My counselor at school, because I...I wasn't eating and couldn't sleep," Ginny said.

"Are you getting any therapy right now?" the doctor asked.

"No, not right now," Ginny answered.

"Fluoxetine has a lot of side effects, like insomnia, nausea and heartburn. You may want to consider some therapy first before taking drugs. It's easy to think you can pop a pill to feel better, but that's not always the case and there are side effects. We have counselors here. Just ask for the business cards of our two therapists at the front desk. You can call or make an appointment before you leave," the doctor said.

"Make an appointment before you leave," Cara said, looking at Ginny.

Ginny just nodded.

Ginny made an appointment for the following week.

When they left Cara said she liked the doctor, that she was no nonsense and practical.

They hailed a taxi even though the clinic was seven blocks from Ginny's apartment. When she got home, Ginny felt weak from the procedure and wanted to rest.

Cara stayed with Ginny until nighttime, making dinner for them with the canned soup she found in the cupboard and some salad at the bottom of the refrigerator.

She left around nine to go home after what was a very, very long day.

Chapter Forty-Seven

Jake knew he was drinking too much, but it dulled his anxiety. He was taking clients out for lunches and drinking, then going home and drinking. He and Stewart were hanging out less often because Stewart was dating someone pretty seriously. Jake sometimes went to a bar on his own now, flirt with women and eat bar food for dinner.

A blood test taken from an annual physical that Tuesday showed that he needed to take cholesterol medication to bring down his numbers. Iris was giving him herbs to help with that, but his numbers were higher than the previous year.

"You're a young man Jake. You have to change your lifestyle or you will not be an old man," the doctor said.

It was two weeks since Jake had spoken to Ginny. He was frantic not knowing what she was going to do. He decided to call and demand to know once and for all what she planned to do.

Jane answered the phone. He heard her cover the mouthpiece and then heard muffled voices. Was Ginny deciding whether to come to the phone? Jesus, he thought, that's rich. She was supposed to let him know and discuss when she would take care of everything, and now she won't even come to the phone.

Finally, he heard Ginny's voice.

"Yes Jake."

"Ginny, I haven't heard from you and you were supposed to let me know..." Jake said not containing his anger.

"It's done Jake. I went for an abortion Friday."

"Ginny, why didn't you tell me?! Goddamn it Ginny! You kept me wondering, kept me worried and all along you were planning to take care of it!" Jake yelled.

"Jake, please stop. I don't need this now." Ginny said and hung up.

After five minutes the phone rang again.

"Sweetheart, I'm so sorry, please let me see you. Can I pick you up tonight? Please, Ginny I've been under so much pressure and I was just so scared. I was scared because you're not ready for this while you're still in school. One day, sweetheart, one day it will be the right time, I promise."

Ginny didn't respond.

"Come on, let me take you to The Coach House where we had our first date. Okay?"

Ginny couldn't say anything. She felt numb. She was still recovering from her abortion, but her strength was coming back. It was Wednesday and on Monday she had had her first therapy session.

"Please?" Jake asked again.

"Fine." she heard herself say.

"Great, plan that I'll pick you up at seven. I'll call for the reservation now. Can't wait to see you sweetheart!"

Ginny hung up feeling emotionally weak.

Jane was in the living room, but Ginny couldn't look at her. Ginny went to her bedroom, shut the door and sat on her bed. She had to see him at some point, she told herself.

Jake hurriedly got dressed. He was pleased with himself. This was good, very good. They could pick up where they left off. They could continue with their routine. He would wine and dine Ginny, they would go to shows, concerts and other fun events. He knew he'd have to make sure she was more careful with her birth control of course. He would insist that she go on the pill now. He thought when he saw her last that her hair was too long. He made a note to tell her he'd send her to that famous hairstylist at Bergdorf Goodman. Everything would be great again and then he could plan. Plan his exit. He would be able to watch her fall in love with him again, to feel her body melt into his as it always had when they made love. Then he could withdraw, slowly at first, then finally he would pull away. If this was going to end, it would be on his terms, when he was ready.

He had to be careful of women like her in the future, conniving to snag him, or get money from him. He was in control again. He looked at his reflection in the mirror as he was leaving and saw his face was getting fuller and the belt had to be loosened one notch. He'll have one less drink tonight and refrain from eating too many burgers at the bar this week.

He hailed a taxi to Ginny's apartment, feeling good that he would call the shots from here on.

Chapter Forty-Eight

84th Street had beautiful brownstones lining both sides of the street from Columbus Avenue to Central Park West. It was a beautiful early Fall evening and the weather was still warm. Cara searched for the number 55 on the buildings on the uptown side of the street. Finally, she saw the brownstone with the large dark stone facade. She walked up the steps and buzzed 4C on the right-side panel. She heard a click and pushed open the door. The entrance smelled warm like old wood with years of polishing. She climbed the stairs and could hear the party before she reached the fourth floor. At the landing she saw the tall blonde.

"Welcome!" Brie said, cheerfully.

Cara walked over and gave Brie a hug and handed over the white wine she brought. Brie thanked her and showed Cara inside.

Cara wore a short green dress and looked around and saw everyone else in jeans and tee shirts. She felt overdressed. There were about ten people there already. She looked around and saw an apartment sparsely furnished, but full of warmth. There were so many colors everywhere. The dining table was blue with yellow painted chairs. The couch in the living room was green with purple, red and orange pillows all over it.

"Come, let me introduce you to everyone," Brie said, taking her hand.

Maria, Walt and Javier came over to hug her, and Cara repeated the names of the other guests as Brie introduced them, hoping to remember them.

Cara went to get herself a plate of chicken salad and vegetables. A woman came up to her.

"Cara, how do you know Brie?" asked a pretty Asian girl.

"Our mother's work together. They are both jewelry designers. That's why Brie is going to medical school and I'm going to be an illustrator. It's a tough business," Cara said, and they both laughed.

"I totally get that. Both my parents are attorneys and I'm an actress."

"Wow, that's fantastic! Are you performing somewhere now where I could see you?"

"Yes, if you want to come to the Carnegie Deli. I perform serving a mean Reuben sandwich! I'm a waitress while I'm going to auditions, hoping for my big break like a million other actors, but I'll let you know when it comes and I'll set aside a Broadway ticket for you, but first, you'll have to remember my name," she said smiling, teasingly.

"Oh please, forgive me, I'm the worst with names. I keep trying all these tricks, but it never works," Cara said, laughing.

"I'm Miranda, Miranda Chen," she said, holding her hand out to shake.

"Nice to meet you Miranda, I'm Cara Jacob," Cara said, shaking her hand smiling.

The evening was fun with more people constantly arriving. Guests were even going out to the fire escape off the living room window to enjoy the warm evening.

The conversation went to old black and white movies everyone had seen. At that point Walt began to recite the famous Marlon Brando scene from *On the Waterfront* perfectly, with hand gestures and the Brando accent.

"You was my brother, Charley. You shoulda looked out for me, just a bit, so I wouldn't have to take those dives for the short end money. You don't understand! I coulda had class. I coulda been a contender. I could've been somebody, instead of a bum which is what I am, let's face it."

Everyone clapped and laughed.

Cara mingled all night with Brie and Maria's friends. Unfortunately, she didn't spend much time with either of them. She did however observe their closeness. They were a team working the room with their guests. At times when Brie was telling a joke, Maria was like her straight man. It was so much fun to watch.

When dessert came out, Miranda brought Cara a slice from one of the pies being served.

"I hope you like apple pie?" Miranda asked.

"Who doesn't! Thank you," Cara said.

"Want to have dessert Al Fresco?" Miranda asked Cara.

Cara nodded.

"Follow me," Miranda said smiling.

Cara followed Miranda out onto the fire escape balancing her paper plate with the apple pie slice. Cara took a deep breath watching the sun going down creating a fiery glow around the rooftops. She could hear the party still inside, but standing there she felt that she had left the world for just a few minutes and she needed that so much right now. Miranda asked Cara about her artwork and asked if she would show her some of her work.

Cara nodded, but felt that Miranda was just being polite. Miranda had such a cool style of dressing, wearing baggy jeans and a black tee shirt that she cut off to be a cropped top. Cara felt so dowdy in her dress.

Later when people were heading home around one in the morning, Miranda asked Cara for her number.

"I'd really like to see your work. I wasn't just saying it," Miranda said.

Cara looked around for a pen and paper and jotted down her number.

As she was leaving Cara gave Brie and Maria a big hug and thanked them for a wonderful evening as she left with the others.

It was the best night she'd had in a very long time.

Chapter Forty-Nine

There was a feeling of sadness as Ginny entered The Coach House. It was almost a year ago that she was here last, but it could have been ten years. She felt like a different girl. Jake thought it would be romantic to take her there again not understanding how things had changed.

Ginny looked around the room that she had admired before and had thought was so beautiful. Now the brick and wood paneling seemed old and dated. They were seated at a red leather banquette that Jake thought was a cozy romantic table that would stir warm memories. Ginny shifted in the banquet and her hand touched a torn piece of the red leather on the seat. She moved slightly away from Jake to avoid snagging her stockings on the tear.

The waiter came by with menus.

"Let's start with some oysters and a bottle of champagne," Jake said.

"Actually, no champagne for me. I'll have a glass of Chardonnay please," Ginny said to the waiter.

"Oh, okay then, cancel the bottle and I'll just have a glass of champagne," Jake said, looking at Ginny with a puzzled look.

"Listen sweetheart, before I forget..." Jake said and reached into his pocket and handed her an envelope with a check. This should cover your expenses for the...you know," Jake said smiling.

Ginny looked at him and handed it back.

"I'm fine. Really, I don't need it," Ginny said, feeling so good about pushing it away. Of course she needed it. She used all her savings to make the "problem" go away. Her mother was sending her a small amount of spending money as usual, but she would have to budget that and use some of it for her therapy co-pays. Yes, Jake's check would help, help a lot, but taking money from him felt sickening. If he wanted to help her during this tough time, he should have been with her, supported her, taken her to the procedure and comforted her.

Jake shrugged and put the envelope back in his jacket.

They both sat and looked over the menu. The waiter came with the drinks and oysters. Jake looked at the menu again to give the waiter the dinner order.

"Steak again for you, as last time?" Jake asked.

"No, the crab cakes," Ginny said.

Jake ordered the steak for himself, added a martini for himself and looked at her.

"You look beautiful tonight, Ginny. You know I love that dress, I'm glad you wore it. By the way, I see your hair has gotten very long. I want to send you to Garren at Bergdorf's. He's done Christie Brinkley and Farrah Fawcett. He'll give you a beautiful new style. I'll have my assistant make an appointment for you."

Ginny smiled, ate an oyster then said.

"Actually, I like my hair the way it is. It's long enough for me to put it up or wear it down. It's a perfect length for me, but thank you."

Ginny looked at Jake. He seemed sad and small for his six-foot tall frame. He was starting to get gray hair and he had put on weight. The handsome man was fading. What struck her was she felt nothing sitting next to him in this old red leather booth. She saw he wanted to rekindle what they had before he panicked and yelled at her for being so irresponsible and conniving. He wanted her back so he could take care of her in the world according to Jake Baines. What Ginny was also feeling was loss, the loss of what she thought would be a wonderful relationship that was trusting and loving. If she stepped out of line in his world, he would accuse and abandon her again. She wondered why she bothered to go to dinner tonight.

The dinner conversation was trite and mostly about Jake's clients and ad campaigns. Ginny listened and nodded. When the dinner plates were cleared Ginny told him she'd skip dessert and that she was tired and needed to get home.

Jake asked for the check. He looked at her and smiled. She smiled back indifferently. Jake saw this and was confused. He thought things would be fine, but this was not going as planned. He understood that she must be tired from her week, but this was something else.

They walked back to her building and at the entrance to her apartment building, Ginny realized he'd never even come upstairs to see where she lived. He'd never met Jane or any of her other friends. Of course not, he wouldn't fit in. He would be sitting with her peers like everyone's daddy who came along as a chaperone. Only he was the one for whom a chaperone was needed to protect her and her peers.

When they arrived at her street Jake turned to face Ginny then leaned in to kiss her. She turned her face so that he kissed her cheek instead. Jake pulled back and looked at her shaking his head.

"Ginny, all night you've been acting strange and not yourself. Now you won't even give me a proper kiss. Come on, I told you I'm sorry and that I was scared. I love you Ginny, please let's just forget everything and go back to being 'us'," Jake said.

Ginny stepped back and stared at Jake.

"Forget everything? Forget that I was pregnant and scared? Forget that you didn't call me for two weeks as I was going through hell? Forget that you never offered to come with me to the doctor? Forget? No Jake, I will never forget," Ginny said, then thanked him for dinner, turned and went into her building knowing it was over.

Jake stood and stared at the front door in disbelief.

Chapter Fifty

Zabar's was busy at four in the afternoon even on a Thursday. Cara checked the shopping list her mother left this morning. The weekly shopping was down quite a bit since Mel had passed.

Connie planned to make her chicken parmigiana that Cara loved. Cara bought the chicken cutlets, tomato sauce and fresh mozzarella. She also picked up salad, and the black-and-white cookies and the lemon pound cake that Connie loved, and which Connie said could only be found at Zabar's, hence the subway ride to shop.

As she shopped, she thought of the conversation with Ginny earlier that day. Ginny had filled her in on her last dinner with Jake, and how much stronger she felt.

Ginny was working with a therapist now whom she liked, and she was learning about herself through discussions of her childhood. She mentioned to Cara how spending so much time with Connie and Mel when she was a child really helped her during those tough times with her parents.

Cara took her wagon to the checkout line, paid and left for the subway uptown.

She was putting away the groceries when Connie came home, walked over and gave Cara a hug.

"Hey hon, guess who will join us for dinner tonight?" Connie asked.

"Who?" Cara asked back.

"Jake! Gosh, it's been ages, and I've been wondering if everything is okay with him. The poor thing works so hard and probably never has a home cooked meal," Connie said.

Cara stopped what she was doing, but didn't say anything. Cara knew this day would come. She would not be able to avoid seeing him. Then there were the holidays that would be coming up. For Thanksgiving, the family usually came from Albany and picked up Connie's elderly aunt, who lived in New Jersey, along the way.

Jake was also always there.

Cara helped her mother prepare the dinner thinking of what she would do when she saw him. Connie took out the dinner plates and set them on the kitchen table humming to herself.

Cara saw how happy her mother was to see her beloved brother. As they both were pulling out the wine glasses, the downstairs buzzer rang. Jake arrived holding two bottles of red wine.

The three of them sat in the living room with cheese, crackers and the wine that Connie had set out on the coffee table. Connie was bubbly and chatty asking Jake about his latest projects and about his trips to Asia for business. Jake seemed tense when he arrived, but happy to see Connie and was starting to relax with his glass of wine. Connie joined him with a glass. Cara refused a glass of wine. She sat next to her mother on the couch while Jake sat in the armchair in front of them. After a while Jake looked at Cara and asked about her classes and her plans after she graduated. He had forgotten all about their past conversation and his offering to help her with an entry level position as an illustrator at Benton & Bowles.

She watched him turn on the charm with her mother, laugh at her jokes, and compliment Connie on her dress even though he'd seen it five hundred times. With Cara he did the same.

"Cara, have you done something new with your hair? It looks great!" Jake said.

"My, you've really grown into a beautiful woman, so smart and talented too!" he added.

Cara continued to watch him, imagining him with Ginny. She tried to envision him taking Ginny to fancy dinners, his favorite concerts, shopping for outfits he'd like to see her in, more dinners, and then to bed. She wondered exactly how he seduced her. Did he get her drunk? Did he slowly touch her or did he just take her straight to bed? It was Ginny's first time with a man, after all. Of course, he turned on the charm with those seductive blue eyes and his smile that lit up his face.

Dinner was ready.

They went to the kitchen and Cara helped bring the food to the table. Another bottle of wine was opened. Connie was still nursing her first glass of wine so Jake had consumed most of the bottle.

Cara watched Jake eating the meal her mother so happily made to feed the brother she loved so much. The brother that she would do anything for. The brother she protected fiercely as a child.

Cara took a small helping of food and picked at it. She had no appetite.

She turned her gaze on her mother who was looking at Jake fascinated in everything he was telling her. Connie laughed at his jokes, smiled when he spoke of his adventures in Hong Kong, nodded in agreement at his opinions on politics. They had the same views. Cara realized then that her mother would never be able to hear that Jake seduced and abandoned that sweet girl who practically lived at their home growing up, or that he made her miserable and hurt her. The worst part was he made Ginny fall in love with him.

Connie and Cara cleared the kitchen table and then they brought the lemon pound cake with small dessert plates into the living room. Connie asked Jake if he'd like coffee and he nodded. She then left the living room to make coffee leaving Cara and Jake alone.

"Did you have fun this summer at Lake George? I wanted to get up there, but couldn't get away with all my work," Jake said.

Cara thought that he really didn't ask a question or care about an answer.

There was an awkward silence. She could hear her mother fussing in the kitchen. She thought of getting up to help her, but decided to stay.

Cara then looked at Jake.

"Uncle Jake, I know what you did to Ginny."

Jake stared at Cara and opened his mouth to say something just as Connie came back in with the coffee.

Jake stayed another hour and then made an excuse that he had a project he was working on and had to leave. Connie gave him a long hug goodbye and Cara said goodbye staring at him from behind her mother.

Chapter Fifty-One

His apartment was dark. Jake only bothered to turn on one lamp in the living room. He walked into the kitchen and opened the refrigerator where the light made him wince. He then reached into the freezer to take out the Limoncello. He took a cube of ice and placed it into a small glass and poured the Limoncello over it. He turned on his stereo and put on David Sanborn's Change of Heart album. He looked at the title on the album cover holding his glass thinking how ironic that was.

He walked over to his leather couch and sat down. The Limoncello was sweet and strong and tasted good going down his throat.

He sat thinking that of course Cara would now know about him and Ginny. How stupid could he be to think otherwise. He was assuming that Ginny would want to keep this all to herself, not to reveal the relationship, their intimacy and the problem that had come between them. He was wrong; he now figured that she must have told Cara everything.

He took another sip of his drink and thought about Ginny. She was not the beautiful young girl that he could help grow into the woman of his dreams. He was no professor Henry Higgins and she was no Eliza Doolittle.

He was glad to see Connie that night. His sister would always see the best in him and would always root for his success.

Cara was another story. He was so hurt by the look in her eyes, there was hatred there without hearing his side. He wanted to talk to Cara, but he wasn't even sure she would hear him. He had done so much for his niece. He spent so much time with Cara when she was a little girl and he had wonderful memories of taking her places and of the whole family having fun together. He was a great uncle and now she was treating him with a cold shoulder.

Jake finished his drink, turned off the light and walked to his bedroom. He switched the light on next to his bed. He then undressed himself completely. He looked at himself in the floor length mirror on the left side closet door. He saw he was getting a bit wider around the waist and some gray was at his temples, but overall, he thought he looked pretty good for a man of forty-six. He stretched his arms above his head and took a deep breath. Then he turned, walked to his bed and lay on the covers naked. He looked at his watch. Eleven thirty. It was still early. He reached for the phone and dialed Iris. She picked up after one ring.

"Talk to me baby. I need to sleep" he said.

"Why don't I just come over?" Iris replied.

"No, I have an early day tomorrow. You know what to do." Jake said.

Chapter Fifty-Two

"Hi Cara, it's Miranda."

Cara buzzed her in.

She had placed her portfolio on the coffee table in the living room and was looking forward to showing it to someone outside of her friends and family.

Miranda came in smiling,

"What a fun area of the city this is with all the students, just like downtown in the village by NYU." Miranda said.

"It's changed a lot since I was young when there were so many SROs and bums around. You got your street smarts quickly as a child growing up here!"

They chatted for several minutes about growing up in the city. Miranda grew up on the East Side in the nineties which was also changing from what it was when she was young.

Finally, Miranda said. "So let me see your work, I've been looking forward to this."

They both sat next to each other on the couch as Cara opened her large portfolio.

Miranda looked at Cara's watercolors of soft landscapes and flowers. As she flipped the pages, amazing drawings appeared combining pen and ink drawings with pastels and watercolor all on the same page. It was as if the images were dancing on the paper. The drawings were so incredibly detailed. They were of people dancing, girls sitting by a river, a boy in a rowboat on a lake, dogs and cats lounging and many portraits of what looked like Cara's mother and father. Miranda was blown away.

"Cara, these are amazing!" Miranda said, looking at Cara.

Cara smiled. "I loved making these. I just hope I can make a living doing what I love. I'd love to illustrate a book one day, but I'll see."

"You will, Cara. You are so talented. Have you contacted any galleries?" Miranda asked.

"Actually no, I didn't think I had enough work for something like that," Cara said.

"I have a friend in my acting class whose mother has a small gallery in Soho that specializes in new artists. She hopes to catch them before they get super famous. Even if you want to illustrate, this could get your work and name out there and then it could lead to connections. My friend's name is Allegra and I'll call her later to have you show her mother your work," Miranda said.

"That is so generous of you. That would be wonderful! Thank you!"

"Don't thank me yet. Let's see what happens," Miranda said, then added, "Hey, this Friday I want to try a new Greek restaurant on Amsterdam and 88th Street. Can you make it? I'll ask Brie and Maria. Maybe Javier, Walt and Allegra can make it too."

Cara said she could join them and felt so good about getting together with all of them again.

Miranda looked at the portfolio. She flipped the pages again and stopped at her favorite images asking Cara which artists inspired her. Cara told her Paul Klee and Georgia O' Keeffe. Miranda asked her if she was inspired at a certain time of day? Cara answered that early morning and late evening were peaceful to her and she could feel the pull to create, and that she especially liked to paint and draw upstate at her country house on Lake George. Cara didn't think she had spoken so much about her work to anyone else before.

They also spoke about Miranda's auditions coming up and about how tough it is to be a struggling actress in New York City. Miranda had performed in some off-off Broadway plays and promised to tell Cara where they would be so she could come.

When Miranda left to go home Cara smiled as she moved her portfolio to the hall table. She went to her kitchen and got a small dish with water. She then took out her sketch pad, watercolor case and paint brush, and started to fill the paper with soft neutral and pastel colors. When she was done, she waited for the paper to dry, then took out her drawing pen and started to sketch over the colors and carefully followed where she had placed the watercolors. After a basic outline was done, she filled in the details, working meticulously.

After some time, she leaned back to observe her drawing of Miranda's face from memory.

Chapter Fifty-Three

Ginny decided that she would fly to Los Angeles for the Christmas and New Year break from school. For Thanksgiving Ginny's mother Barbara was going to a new boyfriend's family so Ginny would join Sara and Sara's boyfriend Adrian at his parent's home in Connecticut.

The Fall semester seemed long and never ending. Ginny had her classes and her therapy once a week with a very reassuring therapist named Theresa Benson. Theresa was kind and soft spoken and was able to get Ginny to open up. She had some tough therapy sessions that dealt with her childhood and fears of abandonment, especially from men. The need to please overwhelmed her own needs. She also started to understand her mother a little better as she spoke to Theresa about her upbringing and her parent's relationship. She was now seeing her mother as a young woman also in fear of abandonment and not knowing what to do with a failed marriage and two young girls. Ginny never learned how to navigate a bad situation in a relationship since there was no role model. She only witnessed fear and the desperation to not be left alone.

She started to call her mother Barbara more often to talk about her courses and to ask her mother how she was doing. She only mentioned Jake to tell her that she was not seeing him anymore, which pleased Barbara. Ginny decided to wait to tell her mother about the abortion.

Ginny had seen Cara a few times over the Fall semester and Cara had invited Ginny to join her and some of her new friends that she had met, but she had declined. Ginny loved Cara and was so grateful for what she did for her during her time of need. Something else was happening though. When she would see Cara, she couldn't help but think about Jake, who she was trying to forget. There were small features on Cara's face like the angle of her nose or her forehead that were Jake's. She would not go to dinner at Cara's right now because seeing Connie would just bring up the lies that she told Cara before, therefore deceiving them both. There was also a chance that Jake might show up which she couldn't stomach. She told herself she needed time. Time to find herself and better understand what she wanted.

She felt Cara too was moving away, getting to know new people and she sounded so happy when she spoke of them. Cara, being Cara, was trying to do what she did in High

School, inviting Ginny to join her with her friends, always making Ginny feel included. This time, Ginny felt she needed to find her own way. She had gotten close to Jane and met friends through her, but even with Jane she felt she needed to hang back from socializing with those friends. It was a need to meet her own friends and have the friendship based on who she was completely, not through an introduction. In her writing classes she found herself talking more to her classmates and even though she didn't socialize after school with them, it was helpful to make those connections. Each time she had an engaging conversation with someone she met on her own, the more she owned that potential friendship and where it would go.

Ginny got on the phone and booked her flight to LAX for Saturday, December 22nd, the day after her last final.

Chapter Fifty-Four

The family from Albany started arriving around 3 pm for Thanksgiving at Connie and Cara's apartment. There were five of them, Mel's younger brothers Larry and Dean, their wives Vicky and Petra. They picked up Connie's elderly aunt Helene on the way down. Dinner would be early since they planned to do a round trip back to Albany that night.

Cara had made the pumpkin and pecan pies the night before, and in the morning, helped Connie with the turkey and side dishes. A table was set up in the living room to accommodate everyone. The coffee table was pushed to one side. They borrowed two chairs from the superintendent in the building to add to their table.

This was the first Thanksgiving without Mel, and it was good to have family around.

When everyone arrived, they pulled the chairs around the front of the couch to face each other to talk. It was tight, but it worked. Everyone asked Cara eagerly about school and what she planned when she graduated. She was happy to share with them her dreams of becoming an illustrator and how determined she was to make her goals happen. Mel's brothers had the same quiet kindness that Mel had and being with them was comforting.

Cara was helping Aunt Helene move from a seat to the more comfortable couch when the buzzer rang. Connie called out to Cara to open the door. Cara's Uncle Dean thankfully came to the rescue offering to get the door since he was close to it.

Cara heard his voice before she saw him. After she finished helping Aunt Helene, Cara turned to see him. Jake seemed to strut in with a swagger. He loved the attention from relatives who he would see once a year and who admired the successful man in New York City. The attention in the room now turned to Jake whom they showered with questions about his work, travels and adventures. Cara sat next to Aunt Helene and didn't stand up when he came in. No one seemed to notice because of the greetings and questions they were asking Jake.

At one point, Jake looked at Cara, smiled and nodded.

Cara looked away.

Dinner was served and everyone found their places around the table. Cara and Connie sat at the end near the hallway so they could get up if anything was needed in the kitchen. Cara avoided looking in Jake's direction as much as possible.

Connie sat next to Cara and raised a glass of wine to toast Mel and all he meant to her. She got weepy and Cara put her arm around her, tearing up herself. Then Jake tried to lighten the mood by telling everyone about some funny things that happened on a trip to Asia. The table started to get lively and Connie seemed happy.

When Cara was clearing the table with her mother, Connie asked her, "Are you okay? I know this must be hard with Mel not here."

"I'm fine, really," Cara said, knowing she should join in the conversation more. She was fine before Jake showed up. Just seeing him made her shut down.

After dinner Connie and Cara brought in the pies and plates. Everyone was laughing at something Jake had told them when they returned to the table. Even Aunt Helene was hysterically laughing. Jake was holding court now after a few drinks. Connie had Jake share the joke and she joined in the laughter. Cara looked down and focused on the pecan pie slice she was cutting to pass around.

Everyone stayed until nine and then everyone kissed and hugged and said their goodbyes. Jake said he would stay and help clean up. Cara offered to walk her relatives to their cars.

After she waved goodbye to the second family car driving away, Cara walked to the Columbia University campus. As she passed through the large open gates on 116th Street, she remembered her father Mel taking her there to play. She used to slide down the embankments on the sides of the stairs, run around the fountains in front of the Low Library building in the summer and run inside them when they were drained for the season. Mel would chase her and they would play tag. She loved those days. She sat down on one of the steps leading up to the library and started to cry. She missed her father so much.

She looked at her watch. She had been gone for about an hour. When she got home, she was relieved Jake was gone. Connie asked where she went because Jake wanted to say goodbye. Cara told her mother she wanted to feel close to Mel and that she went to the campus. Cara started to cry again and Connie came to her and they both held each other.

Chapter Fifty-Five

Ross Banner and Eric Green waited in the conference room at Benton & Bowles offices. They were waiting for Jake to come in. They had discussed with each other what was the best approach to deal with Jake's issue, and finally concluded to face it head on. Jake was a good man and he would take it well and fix the problem.

When Jake arrived, he looked tired, but acted cheerful as he sat across from them.

"Jake, we called you in because some accounts have mentioned that lately, you seem to have a lack of focus for the direction of their campaigns and products," Eric said.

"What? Who is saying this?" Jake asked, irritated.

"Jake, please listen to us," Ross said.

"Some people here have also noticed on client lunches and dinners that you've been drinking rather excessively to the point of making clients uncomfortable. Jake, listen, you have been with us a while now and we value you, but we want you to address your drinking. We're afraid it's affecting your work. We want you to get some help," Eric said.

Jake sat there looking at them and said nothing. How dare they speak to him that way. After all the money he's made for the firm. Sure, he wines and dines the clients and has a good time with them, but it is never to excess, he thought. He wanted to yell at them and tell them off, but instead just said, "Thank you for pointing this out to me. I will speak to someone about this and work on it, not to worry."

"That's great Jake, that's exactly what we wanted to hear," Ross said, as he stood up along with Jared.

"We know you'll do the right thing," Eric added as he patted Jake on the back. They both left the conference room leaving Jake alone.

Jake sat there feeling humiliated. He felt like a little boy being reprimanded for acting badly. He got up slowly and walked to his office. The rest of the day he stayed in his office not bothering to speak to anyone and he left promptly at five to go home.

That night when Jake got home, he pulled out his resume and started to work updating it. He would reach out to headhunters soon to see what they could do for him. Then he went out to his local bar and ordered a hamburger and several martinis.

Chapter Fifty-Six

Kyclades was busy that Friday, but Cara could see Brie, Maria and Miranda sitting at a large table in the far corner. They waved at her and stood up to hug her when she came over. They ordered drinks and then saw Walt and Javier arrive with another woman, who was Miranda's friend Allegra and her boyfriend Kurt.

They congratulated Allegra who had just gotten the role of Natalya Petrovna in an off-Broadway production of *A Month in the Country* by Ivan Turgenev. The play was going to open the following February. Walt and Javier said that they must all go for the opening night of the play.

Cara was seated between Allegra and Miranda.

Allegra turned to Cara just before the food came.

"Cara, Miranda has spoken so highly of your artwork. My mother has a small gallery called The Foster Blanc Gallery in

Soho and I'll arrange a time one evening for you to show her your work if you'd like."

"That would be wonderful, thank you. Miranda was so encouraging, and it will be great to get professional feedback."

"Wonderful, give me your number before we leave," Allegra said.

The food arrived and they asked that all the plates be put in the center and they took turns tasting everything.

The conversation at the table was lively and Cara and Miranda spoke to each other about the latest movies and shows. She could feel Miranda moving closer to her as they spoke. Cara liked the feeling.

At the end of the meal, Miranda asked Cara if she'd like to go for dessert or coffee at a small Italian pastry place nearby.

After dinner everyone hugged and kissed goodbye. Cara gave Allegra her number and Allegra promised to call her the following week.

Cara and Miranda walked to the small Italian café nearby, where they walked down three steps to a huge room with exposed brick walls displaying homemade desserts and offering fresh coffee and tea. Everything smelled so good, and the atmosphere was warm with couches, stuffed armchairs and small coffee tables. Books were placed all around to read or browse if one wanted.

They chose a small corner seating area. Cara ordered a cappuccino and Miranda ordered a chamomile tea and biscotti.

Cara looked at Miranda. She had shoulder length straight jet-black hair and the most beautiful dark brown almond eyes. When she laughed her nose wrinkled just a bit. She was small and slim like Cara and had an eclectic way of putting items of clothing together that was fun and unconventional. That night she wore a baggy top with a slim skirt, combat boots and an armful of black rubber bracelets. Cara loved her look and enjoyed talking to her. Miranda paused at times when they were talking just to look at Cara. This made Cara feel shy, a feeling she was not used to.

Miranda spoke of her family and how difficult it was to be an actress or an artist of any kind in an Asian family.

"You must be a doctor, lawyer, go into finance or anything where you can make a lot of money. Certainly not an actress! In some ways it's easier that I'm a girl. If I were a boy, forget it!" Miranda said.

Her parents were born in China and came here during the cultural revolution. They were conservative as were her two brothers who worked on Wall Street making a lot of money.

"I'm the black sheep of the family," Miranda said laughing.

Cara felt lucky to have her parents who were always so supportive of whatever she wanted to be.

Around midnight they left and walked to the subway. Miranda lived on West 56th Street so she was heading downtown. They both stopped in front of the subway entrance. Miranda looked at Cara, leaned forward and kissed her. It felt so natural to Cara and her heart beat faster as she kissed her back.

When they entered the subway, they could see each other across the platforms in the train station heading in different directions. Cara and Miranda smiled at each other until Miranda's train pulled in. Cara continued to follow Miranda's image until the train pulled away.

Chapter Fifty-Seven

The plane landed on time at LAX airport. When Ginny exited the arrival area, she saw her mother, Barbara, waving at her smiling.

The weather was warm and welcoming and Ginny was feeling good to be in California. Barbara was living in Venice Beach in a small two bedroom she rented one block from the beach. It turned out that Sara and Adrian decided to stay in New York for the holidays so Ginny would have her mother to herself.

As they drove to Venice Beach Ginny looked out the window. Everything looked so bright to her. The streets were lined with bright white or colored houses dotted with palm trees around them. The sunlight seemed to bounce off the sidewalks which looked empty since pedestrians were rare. What a contrast from the cold, gray, busy New York she left behind.

They pulled into the parking area to Barbara's apartment and walked up the steps to her door. Inside wicker furniture with bright colored cushions were placed in the living room, with fun tchotchkes all around. Barbara had put up a small Christmas tree in a corner and it was brightly decorated. The place felt happy and Ginny felt that way too. After Ginny put her things away, Barbara said that she wanted to take Ginny to lunch at a taco place she liked that was right along the beach.

At the restaurant Ginny watched the fun people strolling along the walkway on Venice Beach. As Ginny and Barbara had their lunch, they chuckled at the muscle men pumping iron and commented on some of the crazy outfits that were worn by the people who strode by. It was like an eccentric, crazy parade. Barbara mentioned that David, her new boyfriend who was a producer at Paramount Pictures, was throwing a party for New Year's Eve and asked Ginny if she'd like to go. Normally she would shy away from parties when she didn't know anyone, but as part of her therapy work, she thought it would be good for her to go.

Barbara worked as a wholesale saleswoman and part time model at the dress company called Rarity. She had taken the week off to spend with Ginny driving around Beverly Hills to search for movie star homes, shopping in Santa Monica, lunches in Malibu and Venice, and long drives along the coast. They spent Christmas Day together cooking short ribs and making homemade margaritas and guacamole. They exchanged presents and Ginny asked Barbara if she was seeing David for Christmas later.

"We exchanged gifts last week. David and I both agreed that I should spend Christmas with you alone this year since you haven't met him yet. I was really looking forward to spending time with you." Barbara said, smiling.

"Me too," Ginny said, feeling so happy.

Barbara's boyfriend David had invited Barbara and Ginny to dinner on the Friday after Christmas at The Luau on Rodeo Drive, which was owned by Steve Crane, Lana Turner's husband. David wanted to meet Ginny before his party on New Years Eve. That night Ginny watched her mother getting all dolled up, putting her hair up and slipping into a bright turquoise fitted dress with big hoop earrings.

Barbara looked so happy. She had been dating David for about six months. When they were having lunch one afternoon Barbara told Ginny that David was the first man she knew that completely respected her, always asked her opinions on current events and treated her with incredible kindness. Ginny would hear them on the phone every night before bedtime saying good night to each other sweetly. What a contrast from how her mother was with her father who had made Barbara feel insecure that he was going to leave her. Seeing her mother stronger and more confident was enlightening for Ginny, who had seen her mother as weak and passive all her life.

David picked them up at seven. He was over six feet tall with light brown hair and a big smile. He greeted Ginny warmly and told her he was glad to meet her after he had heard such wonderful things about her from Barbara. Ginny was surprised. She never imagined her mother speaking highly of her to anyone.

They drove to The Luau in Beverly Hills and then entered the famous Tiki palace. They crossed the bridge over the moat surrounding the restaurant. Ginny saw cocktail drinks in coconuts and pineapples on fire! The food looked exotic too. The ceiling was covered with bamboo and palm fronds. Ginny remembered Jake took her once to Trader Vic's at the Plaza, but this was a Tiki Bar on steroids. It was such an exotic atmosphere and Ginny was having so much fun. David asked all about her school and courses and what kind of writing she was interested in doing. He asked Barbara all about their week so far with genuine interest. During dinner, David saw some friends dining at the restaurant waving at him. He waved back, but kept his attention on Ginny and Barbara. After their meals, dessert was ordered and Ginny realized that David never spoke about himself or what he did. So, Ginny asked him.

David said he worked as a producer for films, but was also working on some television shows. He didn't go into much detail. He seemed so humble.

At the end of the night, David drove them back to Barbara's apartment, gave Ginny a hug and kissed Barbara good night saying he'd call her when he got home.

On New Year's Eve at seven thirty, Barbara and Ginny drove to Brentwood to David's home. On the drive there, they passed huge homes that Ginny could hardly see past the iron gates. David's home was a ranch style modern house that was smaller than the other homes they drove by, but it was beautifully landscaped and inside it felt warm and "lived in". David had a deep blue sectional couch with the same bright colored pillows her mother had. Maybe they bought them together, Ginny thought. There was a huge coffee table with stacks of art books. Along the living room wall there was an assortment of unmatched antique side chairs for people to pull closer as the party filled up. There were beautiful pieces of artwork on the blue painted walls that to Ginny's eye had been painted by very established artists.

Barbara and Ginny saw the caterers busying themselves in the open kitchen area. David came over and greeted them both with a big smile and hugs. Barbara wore a black beaded dress and Ginny wore a dress that Jake had bought for her. Barbara and Ginny were the first to arrive because Barbara said she wanted to be available to help, even though it was a catered party. Ginny felt funny just standing around, but soon the guests started arriving. It seemed that her mother knew everyone and quickly and proudly introduced Ginny to the other guests.

One of the women Ginny met that night was an exuberant woman in her fifties named Sandra Phillips, who was a screenwriter who had worked on several film projects for Paramount. She asked Ginny when she was graduating and what she wanted to do.

Ginny was thoughtful and said that she was interested in being a reporter for a newspaper or writing pieces for magazines.

"Have you ever considered writing for movies and television? Paramount is really growing its television division, especially since its acquisition of Desilu. We can always use script doctors in addition to screenwriters at the studios." Sandra said.

"I never thought of that," Ginny said.

"You should come visit Paramount and I'll show you around. I have a small office which isn't very glamorous, but it's fun to see how everything works. How long are you in town for?" Sandra asked.

"Only four more days," Ginny answered.

"Might be tight, but we can try. I'll speak to David. In the meantime, do you have any samples of your writing with you?"

"Gosh no, but I could send you some things," Ginny offered.

"That will work, no worries. Here's my card," Sandra said, finding her purse and producing her business card.

Sandra then introduced Ginny to some other writers who were at the party and the evening flew by. Before Ginny knew it, the countdown to the New Year began.

What a year it had been, Ginny said to herself.

Around one in the morning people started to leave. Barbara was going to stay over and she called a taxi to bring Ginny back to Venice Beach. David and Barbara told her they would pick her up at noon the following day to go for lunch.

That night, Ginny felt great. She was happy with herself for going to the party where she knew no one. She felt herself gaining confidence. She was looking forward to her future.

The rest of the week went by quickly. The day before she was to leave, David had arranged her tour of Paramount studios, and her meeting with Sandra Phillips in her office on one of their lots.

When Ginny arrived, a young woman, not much older than Ginny, greeted her and started a tour of the outdoor film lots and soundstages. Ginny was mesmerized by this world of make believe. There were faux residential neighborhoods, Western towns, Paris streets, and mock railroad stations.

It was also fun to see the cowboys, gangsters, and ladies in long gowns walking by to their sets in their costumes.

At the end of the tour, which took about two hours, she was directed to a small building to the right of one of the sound stages. The screenwriters worked on the second floor. It was a large open area with five desks and Sandra had her own small office off to the left. It was lunchtime when she arrived so only Sandra was there.

"How was the tour?" Sandra asked, smiling.

"It was great! It's really amazing to see how all this works. One just sees a film and doesn't realize how much work goes into making everything come to life," Ginny said.

"Yes, there's a lot behind the scenes," Sandra said, and motioned Ginny to take a seat.

"Let me show another piece of what makes a film come to life," Sandra said, and handed a script for Laverne and Shirley to Ginny.

Ginny looked over the dialogue and directions the actors would be asked to follow. She could picture Penny Marshall and Cindy Williams speaking what was written and could see the story come alive.

"This looks like it would be a lot of fun to be part of this, creating the scripts for the television shows."

"Movies too. Here, let me show you a work in progress for the film Starting Over. You see the revisions and changes here?" Sandra said, pointing to the typed pages all marked up in red and green writing.

"All scripts need to be fine-tuned before they are turned over to the actors. It's great because we bounce ideas off each other here and even act it out to see if it works. We have become a second family here too because we all work closely together," Sandra continued.

"I imagine it's especially great to see your words come to life when an actor delivers them on film," Ginny said.

"Yes, it is. So, Ginny, when you get home send me samples of your writing. We are always looking for talented people here.

It's not like writing for a newspaper or magazine, but if you have the talent, I think you'd enjoy it," Sandra said.

Ginny thanked Sandra and left feeling overwhelmed, but also feeling good about the idea of working in television and film. She hoped her writing samples were good enough to land a job.

The following day, Barbara drove Ginny to LAX for the Red Eye flight to New York. As Ginny boarded the plane, she felt sad to leave.

Chapter Fifty-Eight

Jake arrived at Club Med in Martinique in the early afternoon of December 23rd 1979. Normally he would just go to Club Med for the New Years week, but this year was different. He didn't feel festive this year. He told Connie that work had been so busy that he needed more time away. Connie understood. Iris was another story. Iris seemed upset for the first time since they started seeing each other. He would usually see Iris on Christmas Eve and then see Connie and Cara on Christmas Day with some other relatives who were in town for presents and an early dinner.

Iris had tolerated his need to go away for New Years, but going away for Christmas? It didn't make sense. Jake wasn't talking about work lately or interested in going to the theater or even movies. Instead, he would mope around the apartment when she would come over. Iris had asked Jake if everything was ok, but then regretted it after he snapped at her.

The Club Med in Martinique seemed like the only place on the island that was full of life. There were the houses the locals lived in and some snack shacks and small grocery stores, but that seemed to be it. Jake usually went to Club Med in Cancun, but this year he wanted to try something different. He wasn't pleased. There wasn't a lot to do outside of the club. He spent his days on the beach drinking daiquiris. Sometimes he read the book he brought, but most of the day, he looked around for the lonely looking girl that could use his company.

Finally, he found her. He struck up a conversation with the woman, feigning interest in who she was and what she did. Then as the evening went on and after more drinks after dinner, he invited her to his single room, for which he paid handsomely. The room was sparse, but it served his purpose. He stayed with this woman until she left on December 30th to return home. He promised to call her, knowing he never would. Then the following day a new group arrived for the New Years week and started the hunt all over again for the girl of the week.

The new arrivals came just after lunch. Jake casually watched the women as they came in with their bags. Some seemed like giggling girls which really turned him off. Some were overweight and even though he didn't mind that, he found them usually too insecure and he couldn't be bothered trying to make them feel better about themselves.

"What drink do you recommend at this place?"

Jake turned to see a woman who came up around to his left side. He didn't remember her with the arrival group. She was a perky, full-figured blonde with a wide smile.

"Well, hello there! What's your name, pretty lady?" Jake asked, smiling.

"It's Siobhan, and what's yours, handsome man?" Siobhan asked.

"Jake, at your service. What can I get you? I'm having a daiquiri by the way and they do make a good one here. It's a good way to start your vacation," Jake said.

Jake found out Siobhan had arrived on an earlier flight.

As they sat at the bar, he asked about her name.

"My father is Italian and my mother is Irish. My mother wanted to get some of her country in front of my very Italian last name which is Rossi. Siobhan is a Gaelic name. Mind you my teachers and professors in all my schools never pronounced it properly. Growing up I hated it, but now I love it. Especially when I go to auditions and they have to call my name," she said chuckling.

"Wow, you're an actress?" Jake asked enthusiastically.

"Don't get too excited. I do voice overs and cartoons. I'm a Voice Artist," Siobhan said, sitting up acting proud.

"Because of my heritage I can also do several accents. Go ahead, try me," Siobhan challenged.

"Let's see...how about German?" Jake asked.

"Ohhh that's easy," Siobhan said and proceeded to speak gibberish, but with a German accent. She then went on to do imitations of accents from Hawaii, India, Italy, Australia and The Bronx New York.

Jake was having a wonderful time with Siobhan and she brought him out of his sullen mood.

They went to dinner together and she continued to make him laugh. He told her what he did and she seemed genuinely interested. After dinner, they walked on the beach. Siobhan lived in Westchester, New York. She did much of her work in New York, and came down often. He guessed her age to be mid-thirties, but she had the spirit of someone younger.

Later that night they both went back to Jake's room and made love. Afterward, Siobhan insisted on returning to her own room which surprised Jake. It was not what he was used to.

The rest of the week changed for Jake because Siobhan had Jake join her on boat rides, snorkeling trips, hikes and even dinners out to local restaurants that were actually very good, but places Jake would never have thought of going. He even liked the casual way she approached dressing to go to dinner and her natural look. He was not even sure she wore makeup except for a touch of lipstick. She was so different from other women he had known, and he liked the way he was feeling.

Only on their last night after they made love in Jake's room did she sleep over. Jake held her close all night.

They headed to the airport together and exchanged phone numbers. This time he was going to call.

Chapter Fifty-Nine

It was raining so hard that day that Cara wrapped her port-folio in a large plastic garbage bag and then placed it in an even larger plastic tote bag. Her life's work was here and she couldn't believe it had to rain that particular day.

Cara took the Broadway local train to Times Square, and then switched to the RR to Prince. When she got out of the station, she walked toward Greene Street. She saw the sign for The Foster Blanc gallery, about halfway down the block. She walked to the old factory building and pushed open the heavy metal door.

Allegra had called Cara a few days earlier to tell her she had set up an appointment for Cara to meet with her mother Talia Foster. When Cara entered two women were standing over a desk at the back of the large space that was featuring works of woodblock prints on the walls from an artist named

James Alwin. She looked at the giant canvases admiring the works filled with color.

One of the women turned around and said, "You must be Cara. I'm Talia. Please come in and dry off. What a day!"

"Hi! Thank you so much for meeting with me!" Cara said, not knowing what to do with her wet umbrella. She decided to place it in a corner near the entrance.

Cara went to the desk that they cleared off. Talia introduced the other woman, Geena Blanc, then Talia went to the room behind the desk and grabbed a chair for Cara. The two women asked Cara about her background and what she was studying and working on. Finally, they opened her portfolio and slowly studied her artwork. They took time asking about her medium and what inspired her. Cara was so excited and in awe to be there that she just answered the questions, but didn't elaborate much.

After they finished reviewing Cara's artwork, they told her that the last week of every month they have a group artists show that features up-and-coming artists. Each artist shows two works of art that would be chosen by them to fit in the particular theme of the show. Geena got a Polaroid camera and she and Talia discussed the five pieces they liked of which they would choose two. They then asked Cara if they could photograph them so that they could review the artwork with others to see if they would fit into the next group show. They would call her if her art would make it. Cara immediately nodded and thanked them.

After they were finished Cara packed up her portfolio binder again in the huge black plastic bag and then into the tote bag, and remembering her umbrella, she headed back out into the rain.

As Cara ran to the subway, she heard her name being called. She stopped and it was Jason. Since they stopped seeing each other, they still had a couple of classes together last semester, but because they specialized in different art mediums this year, they had not seen each other. Enough time had passed since their break up that it was becoming less awkward and they hugged. They were both headed uptown and rode the train together.

"I was going to call you. I heard from Matt. He's doing really well and has joined a couple of bands while in college. He mentioned that we should all get together after we graduate this coming Spring. He's been in touch with Lina and she's looking forward to getting together. It will be wonderful to catch up with everyone. I can't believe it's been almost four years since we were all together," Jason said.

"Yes, that would be fun," Cara said, not sure how she felt about it. She had changed so much. She'd mention it to Ginny too although she hadn't heard from her in a while.

Cara and Jason filled each other in on the classes they were taking and then Jason asked why she had her portfolio. She was trying to get her work shown in a gallery. He was visibly impressed. It was a long shot, she explained.

They parted when Jason got off at the 14th Street station and Cara continued uptown.

The rain stopped by the time she got home. She called Allegra to thank her for setting up the appointment with her mother, and filled her in on what had happened.

Then she called Miranda, and they spoke for an hour and made plans to see each other the following day.

Cara slept that night with a smile on her face.

Chapter Sixty

The Spring semester was going very well for Ginny. She was feeling good about her classes. She had sent samples of her writing with a cover letter to the screenwriter Sandra Phillips and was waiting to hear back.

She spoke to her mother more often now and her mother mentioned that she and David had spoken about living together and that she would move in with him that summer. Barbara then invited Ginny to come out and stay in the Venice apartment after graduating, if she wanted, and look for jobs in LA.

Ginny was thrilled. It would do her good to leave New York. She wanted a fresh start and wanted to make new friends. She missed Cara and she knew she had to respond to Cara's requests to get together. She wasn't sure what Cara was going through, but felt indebted to Cara for being there for her.

Her roommate Jane now had a boyfriend, so she wasn't around much. Ginny had the apartment to herself this last semester most of the time. She spent the time writing short stories and going to movies alone. She would never think of going to a movie alone in the past.

She learned to enjoy her own company. She was still seeing a therapist, but cut it back to only twice a month. She was understanding more and more about what she needed even though she wasn't sure yet how to get it.

Chapter Sixty-One

Jake thought he'd wait a week before calling Siobhan. After all she should know he was a busy man with other things to do and other people to be with since he's back home.

He was busy at work and the agency now wanted him to handle the Anheuser-Busch account. He would be traveling to St. Louis, and no longer needed to oversee anything in Hong Kong. He knew this was a demotion. He reached out to recruiters several times, but nothing came up that suited him, so he bided his time being friendly and engaging with everyone at work.

He thought of Siobhan and how much she made him laugh when they were together. She had the skill to draw him out and encouraged him to do things he never expected to do the week before on his vacation. He loved snorkeling in the sea with her. The hikes they took were adventurous and fun. They brought packed lunches the Club made for them and they would stop and wade in the water before and after their meal. She was full of life and also enjoyed a good drink which was great for him. The sex was raucous and passionate and left him wanting more. Maybe he could have a real relationship with her, he thought.

He felt his time with Iris had run its course. It had been almost three years since they started seeing each other. Yes, she was easy going, never questioning, never quarreling, except when she gave him grief about going away for Christmas. It was his time and he could do what he wanted. He hated when women became clingy.

That was something he felt he would never get from Siobhan. She seemed very independent, but loving as well. During their week together, she would kiss him passionately before leaving to go back to her room. That last night when she stayed with him the whole night, he loved holding her and felt close to her, and he was sure she felt the same way.

It had been a week and he was thinking of where he would take Siobhan to show her a good time when they would get together. Maybe Lutece or La Grenouille or La Côte Basque? He wanted to make sure she knew who he was. He even planned what suit he would wear the night they went out.

The work day ended and Jake happily strolled home. He made himself a drink and relaxed until seven, which he decided was a good time to call someone new in your life. Not too early yet still before dinner time.

He pulled the paper out of his wallet with Siobhan's phone number.

He dialed and waited. After four rings an older woman's voice answered. Maybe she lives with her mother? he thought.

"Hello, my name is Jake. I'm a friend of Siobhan. Is she available?" Jake asked, cheerfully.

"I'm sorry, but I think you have the wrong number. There's no Siobhan here," the old lady said.

He felt so silly. He must have misdialed. He looked at the numbers closely and said the numbers softly to himself as he dialed again.

"Hello?" the old lady asked again.

Jake apologized and hung up.

He stood looking at the piece of paper for a long time with the numbers Siobhan had written.

Maybe her name wasn't even Siobhan, he thought.

Chapter Sixty-Two

On Saturday Cara turned right on 56th Street and headed to Miranda's apartment. Cara and Miranda had been seeing each other now for about a month. She climbed the three flights in the dark brownstone and saw Miranda standing in the doorway to her apartment. Miranda's apartment was a small studio decorated with a mix of Asian and contemporary art, big bean bag chairs and Navajo rugs.

She gave Cara a long kiss when she arrived.

Cara dropped her bag and turned to Miranda.

"I have some great news to share. I heard from Talia Foster this morning. She said that my art pieces would not work with the group exhibit next month, but would be perfect for the group exhibit at the end of April! They chose two pieces to be in the show and I'm so excited!" Cara said, practically jumping up and down.

"Oh my God, that's so wonderful! We'll have to tell Allegra when we see her later, but I'm sure her mother already told her," Miranda said.

They were going to the opening that night of Allegra's performance as Natalya. Miranda remembered to pick up roses to give to Allegra after the show.

The performance started at seven and all their friends were going to be there.

Just as the play was about to start Brie and Maria rushed in mouthing "sorry we're late."

The play was set in modern times, instead of the nineteenth century. Allegra played the headstrong Natalya beautifully, and her facial expressions of boredom were priceless. She was very convincing, and moved beautifully on stage. The play was well done even if some of the other actors seemed to overact a bit. Watching their friend's performance was exciting. Cara and Miranda held hands throughout the play feeling good just being there together.

After the play they all went backstage to congratulate Allegra. Allegra looked so happy and was thrilled everyone came opening night. Talia invited all of Allegra's friends to join their family at an Italian restaurant, where they reserved a room for a late dinner and drinks.

Cara and Miranda stayed close to each other along with Brie and Maria since they didn't know anyone else there. Meanwhile Walt and Javier were mingling amongst Allegra's family, chatting with them and making them laugh. Brie looked at them and told Cara and Miranda how Walt and Javier can go anywhere in the world and make new friends. Maria laughed and nodded in agreement.

At the end of the evening Allegra congratulated Cara on being chosen to join a group show at the gallery in April. Talia said she thought both of Cara's pieces would sell. She couldn't believe how supportive Talia was, since some of her professors had told her how brutally tough it is to show in a gallery.

Around one in the morning, Cara and Miranda said good night to everyone and took a taxi uptown to Miranda's apartment.

"What a wonderful evening!" Miranda said.

"Yes, it was. It was even more wonderful to be there with you!" Cara said and she pulled Miranda to her and kissed her.

They made gentle love that night and slept until noon the following day.

Chapter Sixty-Three

Ginny exited the subway station and walked toward Greene Street. She was so happy for Cara when she called and told her about the art exhibit and the opening at the gallery where some of her art would be shown. Ginny had not seen Cara for months and felt terrible about making excuses that she was either busy with school work or that she had other plans.

Ginny entered the gallery and saw so many people there. Twenty artists were represented that night and she had trouble seeing the art through the crowd.

She saw Connie near the entrance and went over and hugged her. Connie asked how she was doing and said she missed her coming around. They spoke a bit more about the show and how talented Cara was. Ginny promised to come for dinner soon and then Connie was pulled away by another visitor.

Ginny worried that Jake might be there, but saw no sign of him.

She stood to one side to search for Cara and finally found her, but she was speaking to a couple of people and she didn't want to interrupt them so she walked up to the table where they were served wine and appetizers. She took a glass of white wine and walked around the show. There were many large canvases and a couple of sculptures on pedestals along a wall. Then she finally saw the two works she knew were Cara's. They were two paintings, one with a little girl dancing in a field where bright shades of watercolor swirled around her finely drawn figure in black and white. There was a card next to it with a description of the mediums used and the title named "Happiness" Then there was a landscape painting that Ginny knew was Lake George. The painting was an acrylic and showed the lake with a few dotted houses along the sides and a small row boat just off the side to the right that Ginny knew was the family boat. This was called "Solitude". She was standing back admiring the paintings when she heard Cara's voice.

"Do you like them?"

Ginny turned around and gave Cara a big hug.

"Oh my God Cara, they are beautiful! You are so talented and to be in this gallery is so amazing." Ginny said beaming.

"Thank you, let me introduce you to the people who have helped with this," Cara said, and started to walk around the gallery searching for Talia and her other friends. Ginny looked at Cara ,whose hair had gotten longer. She styled it with the back pulled up and she left small red curls framing her face. She looked beautiful and very happy.

Cara introduced Ginny as her best friend, and it only made Ginny's heart sink. Ginny was introduced to the gallery owners, Talia and Geena, then to Cara's friends. Ginny realized that Cara was part of a whole new social scene. They were all very friendly, and spoke to Ginny as though they knew her as well, saying that Cara had spoken a lot about her. Javier even took Ginny by the hand to show her around. She spoke awhile with the woman who graduated from NYU, and the woman said how it had changed in the ten years since she had been there. And then the woman went on to say how important the city was in supporting and influencing artists. Ginny didn't quite agree, but just nodded and didn't say anything. Ginny thought that most artists in New York had to have a lot of grit and determination to make it, and that it was very difficult.

Ginny glanced across the room to see Cara with her arm around Miranda and then holding Miranda's hand for a long time. Ginny could see the chemistry between them.

Ginny viewed Cara's work again, and saw the red dots at the bottom of the name cards, indicating that they had been sold.

The gallery was starting to empty out. Cara asked Ginny to join her and her friends at Odeon. Ginny felt her old awkwardness come back. She thought of fighting it and going, but this time she felt it was right for her not to join them and leave Cara to enjoy her moment with her new friends.

They said goodnight to each other and hugged, promising to see each other again soon.

Chapter Sixty-Four

Jake thought of going to Cara's gallery opening that Connie had begged him to attend, but he made excuses. He would go another day that week while the group show was still on, but he wasn't in the mood for Cara's glares. He knew he should speak to her, but fell short of how to approach it and what to say.

Jake had an interview with the William Esty agency at the beginning of the week, and he was hoping to hear back from them by next week. He knew his days at B & B were numbered. He hated going to St. Louis and his enthusiasm for his work was waning. He needed to join a new firm and have a new start. He was feeling his age too. After his annual visit, his primary doctor scolded him for his eating habits and lack of exercise. He thought that he would start running in Central Park. The weather was getting warmer, and he could start slowly.

It was Saturday around six and Iris was on her way over. Jake was seeing Iris every other week now and keeping his options open on alternate weekends and during the week. He wasn't sure when he should end it. She seemed to be fine with the change of dates and still never questioned or complained. She even was telling him about new herbs that could help with his cholesterol. He teased her about her "Voodoo Medicine" as he called it.

He was getting to know some of the new hires at work, but they were so young that he could be their father. He knew they were looking at him as the old man at the company even if he was just in his mid-forties.

He thought that he would take a week of vacation and go to Lake George the following month. He hadn't been there in a year. He pulled out a calendar and turned to May and saw he had written down that Cara's graduation was on Friday, May 23rd. That was in a month. He would send a present and make some excuse that he had a business trip. Connie would be upset, but she would forgive him.

The doorman buzzed him that Iris was on her way up.

He opened the door and she walked in wearing a short slim skirt and fitted sweater. She looked fit and healthy.

Iris put her overnight pouch down and went into her purse and pulled out a bag containing Red Yeast Rice.

"You must take these," she said, smiling and approaching to give him a kiss.

"Sweetheart you know I don't believe in these," Jake said, holding her hand.

"Jake, I care what happens to you. You know I love you," Iris said.

Jake dropped her hand and turned to walk to the bar and poured two vodka tonics.

"Iris, sweetheart, you and I have been so good together for a long time, but..." Jake stopped.

"Jake, no more words, please. Take your drink to the bedroom," Iris said as she took his hand and led him to his bedroom and started to undress.

Chapter Sixty-Five

Miranda was getting dressed and fussing with her hair.

"You look beautiful. There's no more that needs to be done," Cara said, looking approvingly at Miranda.

Cara was also slipping into her new green and black dress, and black heels. Her cap and gown lay on the bed, and Cara bent over to touch it. She couldn't believe how quickly four years had flown by.

Miranda replied, "My mother says that about ten years flying by!"

"Ughh something to look forward to." Cara said.

"This, coming from the artist who is going to have her own show in the Fall!" Miranda shouted back.

After the sales of Cara's two pieces of art at the group show, Talia Foster and Geena Blanc called her about working this summer on some larger pieces to add to her collection, and that they would like her to have a solo exhibit of her work in September at the gallery.

The intercom buzzed and it was Connie. Cara had been staying at Miranda's place for a few days, and Connie was picking them up to head downtown for the graduation ceremony. Connie came in holding a small gift bag.

"Oh Cara, you look so beautiful! I wish Mel could see you now," Connie said.

"Me too. I miss him all the time, but today I especially feel his absence."

"Well, maybe this will bring a smile to your face." Connie said, as she handed Cara the small light blue gift bag.

"What's that?" Cara asked.

"Cara, it's from Jake. He can't make it to the graduation, but he dropped this off for you two days ago. We had dinner together and honestly, I'm worried about him. He looked so tired and I don't think he's physically well," Connie said.

"Have you spoken to him about what could be going on?" Cara asked.

"No, but I'll try soon. You know how he is though, never wanting to bother anyone with his needs. Hey, open your gift. Let's see what he gave you." Connie said excitedly.

Cara reluctantly took the little blue box with the white ribbon around it and opened it. Inside was a beautiful pair of pearl earrings.

"Oh my gosh!" Connie said.

Miranda looked at them and nodded in agreement that they were indeed really beautiful.

"Well, you must wear them today, and call and thank him."

Cara looked at her mother. Connie was so pleased that her brother had sent such a wonderful present on this important day.

"Hey look, there's a card," Miranda said, pointing at the bottom of the bag.

Cara reached in and opened the card.

It read:

To My Dearest Cara on her special day. Went to the Foster Blanc Gallery and saw your work. Your paintings are amazing! You have always been, and always will be very special. Happy graduation and congratulations! Love, Jake

Cara's eyes started to fill with tears. Connie thought it was because Cara was so touched by his thoughtfulness, but it was because Cara felt such an intense loss. She reluctantly put on the earrings, feeling awkward about it.

The graduation ceremony for The School of Visual Arts was at Radio City Music Hall on Sixth Avenue.

When they arrived, there were so many people spilling out into the street that they were blocking traffic. Jason joined them to say hello with his family. Other friends from her classes waved at her.

It was a long ceremony, given that it was a small graduating class.

When Cara Jacob's name was called, she walked on stage and she could hear her mother and Miranda's claps and cheers.

Afterward they went to lunch at a small French restaurant called Adeline on 52nd Street. Cara watched her mother asking Miranda about her acting, and which books she was reading. The conversation flowed easily and they stayed at the restaurant until about three in the afternoon.

Later that night, back at Miranda's apartment later, Miranda asked Cara about the earrings from her uncle. Miranda had seen Cara's face change when she received the gift and read the letter.

"The letter from your uncle sounds so sweet, and the gift is amazing, but you seemed so troubled by it," Miranda said.

"It's a bit complicated. Have you ever seen Hitchcock's *Shadow of a Doubt* with Theresa Wright and Joseph Cotton?" Cara asked.

"Jesus! Your uncle's not a serial killer, is he?" Miranda joked.

"No! It's just that I loved him so much as a child and always looked up to him. When I got older, something happened to change how I see him and I haven't really dealt with it properly," Cara said.

Cara then went on to explain what happened with Ginny and Jake's abandonment of her. She explained that her uncle being in a relationship with her best friend and being secretive about it was bad enough, but the way he treated Ginny was horrible, and so far, she just hasn't gotten past it.

"Cara, yes, he sounds like a shit, but he is your family and it sounds like you need to speak to him. Has Ginny moved on?" Miranda said.

"Who knows, I think so, but doesn't that emotional abuse stick around for a while?" Cara asked.

"Perhaps, but you are not Ginny and you've got to deal with this for your own sake."

"You are right, but right now I want to enjoy my night with you," Cara said, taking both of Miranda's hands.

That night Cara decided she would call Jake to thank him, and to set up a date so they could talk.

Chapter Sixty-Six

The phone rang in Ginny's apartment. It was Sandra Phillips.

"Ginny, we received your writing samples and we think they are very good. We'd like to offer you a job as a Television Script Assistant. The annual salary is ten thousand. You would work alongside my right-hand person, Jill Brody, who has been with me for years. You'll learn the ropes from her. You can start at the end of June which should give you time to get settled here. This must sound overwhelming, so take your time and let me know by the end of May. Is that okay with you?" Sandra asked.

Ginny tried to collect her thoughts.

"Miss Phillips, thank you so much! I don't have to think about it. I'm so excited to be part of your team!" Ginny said, jumping up and down.

"Ginny, fantastic! Welcome aboard. We will confirm your start date soon. There's only one thing, call me Sandra, not Miss Phillips. We are not formal in our office. We are family."

"I am so looking forward to starting! Thank you!" Ginny said.

Ginny hung up, in disbelief.

Barbara and Sara both went to Ginny's graduation. Her father sent flowers. Ginny was understanding the limitations of some people through her therapy sessions, and to choose whether to accept or to dismiss them. Ginny had seen her father fail her mother so many times, she felt that this was just another time. He was still her father, but she decided that going forward she would deal with him on her own terms. She would move on as her mother Barbara had done. Ginny told Sara and her mother about the job offer. Barbara was thrilled that she was moving to Los Angeles and repeated that Ginny could stay in the apartment. The timing was perfect with her moving in with David this summer. She wasn't sure, but Ginny detected some jealousy from Sara. After so many years of being an outsider with her mother and sister, it felt so good to be close to her mother.

Ginny knew that Cara had also graduated the week before, so she decided to call to congratulate her, and try to get together before her move to Los Angeles the following week.

After seeing Cara at the gallery, Ginny realized she had become removed from Cara's new life. The movement away from Cara was of her own making.

When she spoke to Cara, they agreed to meet for lunch at a small Greek restaurant near Columbia University. When Ginny arrived, Cara was already sitting at a table.

"So, we are all done! We got there!" Cara said, after hugging Ginny hello.

"I must say, it feels great to have graduated! And Cara, I was so impressed with the showing you had at the gallery. I saw the red dots showing you sold both pieces too!"

"I'm so glad you could make it to the show. It has been amazing."

Cara then went on to tell Ginny about the show she will have in September and that she must come to see that as well.

"I'll certainly try, but I've been offered a job in California and I'll be moving there next week." Ginny said sheepishly. She wasn't sure why she was acting like that, as though she were abandoning Cara by leaving after all these years of friendship.

"My God Ginny, that's wonderful!" Cara said, genuinely happy for Ginny.

Ginny proceeded to tell her about the job, and that she would take over her mother's apartment sometime in the summer and look for a roommate to help with the rent. She also told Cara that her relationship with her mother was getting better after all the years of emotional distance.

Ginny then looked at Cara. She wanted to ask about Miranda. After observing them at the art gallery, she wasn't sure how to approach asking if they were a couple. So, she just asked "Miranda is very charming. How did you meet?"

"We met at a party that Brie and Maria threw a while back. Miranda and I hit it off right away," Cara said, then looked Ginny squarely in the eye and said smiling, "Yes, we are a couple!"

Ginny laughed. "Okay, I thought so, but..."

"I understand. I struggled with how to deal with what I knew was going on with me. Truthfully, being with Jason cemented it. Something wasn't right, and I knew what it was. I just had to admit it to myself," Cara said, looking at Ginny, remembering all the feelings she had for her.

"I'm so happy for you. Miranda seems wonderful. It's so difficult to sort out our needs and desires and it takes time. My own mother is just figuring this out, and she's fifty!" Ginny said laughing.

They continued to talk about their plans for the near future.

After lunch they strolled through Columbia University's campus remembering playing there as children. The fountains were on and the campus was in full bloom. They watched some children running around the fountains and sliding down the embankments on the sides of the steps laughing and yelling. They saw themselves in them.

They walked slowly to the subway and hugged each other for a long time, promising to call often. Then Ginny disappeared into the dark hole that was the subway entrance. Cara walked slowly back to her apartment.

Chapter Sixty-Seven

Jake drove to Lake George feeling good. Just before he left, he had gotten a call from William Esty. He was offered the job as Account Manager for MasterCard. He would be working in New York only, and that was fine with him. He would start in June.

This was going to be a new start for him. He would meet new colleagues and have new responsibilities. He would also start working on his health and try to develop healthy relationships.

He had taken the week off that he definitely needed. He spent his days at the cabin waking up early and going for walks before breakfast, then in the afternoon he took the row boat out onto the lake for a couple of hours. He loved the quiet of the lake in the Spring before the Summer crowds arrived with their motor boats and kids.

One day Jake drove to the little dirt parking area his parents had driven to near the house. He hiked the small trail covered in pine needles to the open area which was Calves Pen. He looked down at the rocks that formed a shelf above the water. He remembered as a child how Connie helped him get his confidence to jump in.

He went to Vincent's for dinner and ordered a couple of dinners to go for the following nights. He brought some good books to read and decided to spend his nights reading. He didn't go to Topps once that week. There was only wine at the cabin so he had a glass with dinner and did not go to buy vodka, as he would in the past.

One night when he was in the living room, he spied the old family photo album on the lower bookcase. He pulled it out and started flipping through the pages smiling at the photos of his parents and of Connie as a little girl. He thought Connie just got taller, but looked the same. As he continued to turn the pages, he saw the sad overweight boy who never smiled when his photo was taken. As he grew into adolescence his skin became ravaged with acne and he remembered not wanting to go to school, but those darn school photos still had to be taken. The pain returned to him. He continued to turn the pages and saw more photos of himself. He realized that all these pictures of him were prominently placed in the album next to his beautiful sister. The photos were not shoved in a pocket of the album or placed in the back somewhere. They were front and center. He saw how even though he felt ashamed of his looks and felt awful about himself, his parents did not. They were proud of him and showed off his photos for everyone who looked at this album to see. They never saw his baby-fat or bad skin; they saw only the son that was loved. He put the photo album away and sat quietly for a long time.

As he drove on the highway back to New York, he decided he really had to speak to Iris. Yes, they had amazing chemistry, but there was no real future. He knew she'd understand. She was such a good sport about so many things.

He also needed to speak to Cara. Connie had called to thank him for the graduation gift. She said Cara would call, but he hadn't heard from her. He told himself he had been away so of course he hadn't heard from her. He wanted to clear the air with her. He needed to for everyone's sake.

As he drove into his garage to park, he brightened up. This was going to be a fresh start for him.

Chapter Sixty-Eight

Cara tried calling Jake several times at his apartment. She then tried his office and they told her that he had taken a week off. She made a mental note to call him in a week or send a thank you note. Maybe that would be best, she thought, I'll send a thank you note, this way there would be no confrontation. She then remembered Miranda's words and realized that she was being ridiculous. She had to deal with the strained relationship and speak to him.

She was busy buying materials for her new art pieces at Pearl Paint on Canal Street that Tuesday. She thought of working on some collages in addition to her usual drawings and paintings. She picked up fresh watercolors, larger brushes, canvas rolls, and paper mache'. She would go to a small lumber yard on West 88th Street to get the wood for the frames. She was so excited to get started.

Cara returned home carrying two large bags of art supplies. When she entered their apartment Connie was home.

"Cara, have you reached your Uncle Jake to thank him for the earrings?" Connie asked frantically.

"Relax, please. I've tried several times at his home and finally I called his office and they told me he was on vacation. I'll try him again tomorrow," Cara said.

"I just got a call from his office saying he was supposed to return to work yesterday and he never showed up or called. They had my phone number as an emergency contact. I tried him at home and there's no answer," Connie said, concern in her voice.

Cara saw the look on Connie's face, and said, "I'm sure he's fine, but since you are so worried, do you want us to go and check on him?"

"I think so. Let me try him one more time at home," Connie said, and dialed Jake's number. It just rang and rang.

"Let's jump in a taxi over there. If we look like fools, so what! I won't be able to sleep tonight without knowing he's okay," Connie said, grabbing her purse.

"Maybe he's just not feeling well or had too many drinks," Cara said, then saw her mother's disapproving look.

"I'm sorry. I'm sure he's fine," Cara said again.

They hailed a taxi to go across town to Jake's apartment building. It was rush hour and traffic was heavy. Each traffic light felt like an hour. Connie became fidgety. Cara took her hand. When they finally arrived, the doorman opened the taxi door. Connie told the doorman that she was Jake Baines' sister and to please call up to Jake's apartment. They waited and waited.

Connie asked if he had seen Jake today. The doorman said he didn't know because he had only come on duty at 4:00 pm. The doorman offered to call the superintendent of the building. Again, they waited. The superintendent came out of an elevator and asked what they wanted. Connie explained that no one has heard from her brother in a couple of days and they wanted to make sure he's all right. Cara stood there, so helpless. Her mother was pacing and insisting the superintendent please get a key to check. Finally, he relented.

As they rode the elevator with the superintendent, Cara suddenly felt dread. The worry that had all seemed ridiculous before, became real. Her mother was always fussing over Jake. To Cara, Connie was always overly proud, overly exuberant. overly concerned, but now Cara knew something wasn't right.

The superintendent slowly opened the door.

"Mister Baines?" He called out.

"Jake?" Connie called out behind him.

They pushed the door open further and slowly walked in. Cara followed, but hung back.

The living room was empty as was the kitchen area. Everything seemed in its place. Cara looked around the living room and saw the black couch that she remembered from his old apartment. Everything else was new to her. Why hadn't he invited her here? Even Connie had only come a few times.

They continued to call his name. They walked into the bedroom which was tidy and clean. It was empty too. Connie then turned to step into the bathroom when she saw Jake's shoes from just behind the door. She walked further in then she saw Jake lying on the bathroom floor, fully clothed, as if he had just come home. She screamed his name and ran to him. He was face down, not responding. She was trying to turn him over, but couldn't. The superintendent leaned in to help. Cara stood behind her mother in disbelief.

They tried to revive him, not knowing exactly what to do. Connie was on her knees pressing down and then releasing, as she thought she had seen people do on television for heart attack victims.

Then the superintendent put his two fingers on Jake's neck.

"Miss, I'm so sorry, it looks like he's gone," he said.

"NO! Please call an ambulance! He can't be gone!" Connie yelled.

Cara stared at Jake lying there, looking as though he were sleeping. Was this a heart attack or a massive stroke? She knew his blood pressure and cholesterol were high. Connie had told her. She went down on her knees and leaned over to hold her mother.

Then the superintendent lifted the walkie talkie from his belt and called the doorman to call 911.

"PLEASE call an ambulance! We can save him!" Connie yelled.

"Miss, please understand, the emergency call will send paramedics and they will take him to a hospital and determine everything," he said gently. The superintendent's face looked ashen. It didn't seem as though he had ever dealt with this before.

Connie wouldn't leave Jake's side. She was sobbing. Cara felt so helpless.

The emergency unit arrived and examined Jake. After a minute with him they pronounced that he indeed had passed away. Connie cried louder.

They said they still had to take Jake to the hospital to have a doctor officially examine him, and an autopsy would most likely need to performed to determine the cause of death because he had died alone. It would take about a week. Connie just nodded. They asked Connie for her phone number to contact her. Cara gave them the number. They then handed Cara the phone number of the coroner's office. They asked if he had any health issues. Connie nodded, but couldn't speak.

"He had high blood pressure and high cholesterol," Cara said.

The paramedics looked around the bathroom and found some prescriptions and said they needed to take these for the coroner.

"Do you have his ID? A passport or driver's license will do," one of the paramedics asked Cara.

Cara left the bathroom and looked around the bedroom and finally found Jake's wallet in his nightstand. She took out his Driver's license and handed it to the paramedics. They then asked Cara to take her mother to the other room.

Cara went to her mother and lifted her up and brought her to the living room. They sat for several minutes on the couch as they heard the paramedics preparing to take Jake away.

Cara made sure that Connie faced Cara and not the door as they carried Jake out in the body bag. The superintendent followed.

Then Cara took Connie by the hand and went down to the lobby. The doorman offered his condolences to them both, then hailed a taxi.

When they got home, Connie went to her room to lie down.

Cara went to her own room to finally cry.

Chapter Sixty-Nine

It was determined that Jake died from a massive heart attack. After the coroner's office called, Connie made the decision to have him cremated.

Cara took care of the funeral arrangements and Connie phoned relatives to let them know about Jake. Cara called the number that Ginny had given her in Los Angeles, but Ginny's mother Barbara answered. Cara left the message asking her to tell Ginny that Cara's Uncle Jake had passed away. Barbara said that she was genuinely sorry and would let Ginny know.

Cara watched her mother fuss about what she would wear to the funeral. Connie even stressed about how Cara was going to wear her hair that day.

"No, no pull it back. It looks so much better that way," Connie ordered.

Cara pulled it back.

It had been a couple of days since Cara had left the message for Ginny about Jake. She started to wonder if she didn't get the message. Then she thought of what Ginny went through with Jake so why should she call? She was probably still angry or upset, or who knows what. Cara was disappointed that Ginny hadn't called Connie or her just to say something. She wondered how often she would speak to Ginny now that Ginny had moved to the West Coast. She knew friendships change with distance. Maybe she would never hear from Ginny again.

Cara and Connie went downstairs at the time the car service was to arrive, and they were happy to see the black town car already in front of the building. They sat in silence in the back seat as it drove toward Riverside Memorial Chapel.

Once inside, Cara saw the photo of Jake that she had enlarged earlier that week. It had been placed on an easel by the entrance. The only photo Cara could find was one taken ten years ago. He looked so handsome in it that Connie said it was fine as a display photo for that day. He also looked so happy.

Cara ushered her mother inside and they took their seats in the front row. The pedestal with Jake's ashes was directly in front of them along with a podium.

Family and friends started to arrive and offered condolences. Cara's friends came, and Cara introduced them to Connie. Miranda hugged Cara and Connie. Miranda motioned to Cara that they would take seats in the back so the family could sit up front with them. A few minutes later, Jason came over with his mother, whom Cara and Connie had met only once at the high school graduation. Cara was touched that they would come.

After everyone found seats, the funeral director approached the podium. Riverside Memorial had asked Cara to write some information and some fun anecdotes about Jake. She was thrown by that request, so she asked Connie. Now she heard this stranger saying what was basically written by Connie. Cara hated it.

Connie went to the podium to read a poem that she liked, called *Afterglow.* Connie had asked Cara if she wanted to say anything at the funeral, but Cara declined.

As Cara listened to her mother, she thought that she should have said something about the fun she had with Jake as a child and how he always made her laugh. She could have brought up the time she and Ginny were so anxiously waiting for their results from their Music and Art exams, that he took them to the movies and for ice cream to take their minds off it, or all the times he took the time to play games with her as a child when he could see that she was bored. She could have stood up and said all of those things.

It was too late now.

After the funeral service, family and close friends went to an Italian restaurant called Gino's on 78th Street and Columbus Avenue. They had a private room in the back, which Connie had reserved for lunch.

Cara's friends hovered around her, and Miranda held her hand. Cara noticed some family members eyeing Miranda with her, but Cara didn't care, especially today.

The lunch was very touching, and it was there that people stood up to tell stories of Jake. Some were funny and some were sentimental.

Cara finally felt the time had come for her to say something. She stood up and tapped her glass. She told the story of how Jake tried to convince Cara that dolphins lived in Lake George, and that he had never complained about enduring so many games of *Candyland* and *Chutes and Ladders* to make her happy. As she stood there speaking, her throat started to choke and her eyes began to tear. Connie stood up, came to her and hugged her. When Cara sat back down, Miranda, who was sitting next to Cara, put her arm around her.

When Cara and Connie finally returned home, they were exhausted. The restaurant packed leftover food for them to take home. As they were putting the food containers in the refrigerator, the phone rang. Connie was closest to the entrance to the kitchen and went to pick up the phone in the hall.

Cara continued to put the food in the refrigerator and listened to Connie talking about the funeral and how moving the service was. She also spoke about how great the luncheon was that day. She told the caller about the family and friends who came and even some friends whom she hadn't seen in a while. Then she asked the caller how they were and what they were doing and then her mother just listened for a long time.

Cara had put all the food away and cleaned the kitchen table. She then poured herself a glass of water and was heading to her room when she heard her mother say, "Hold on, she's right here."

Connie walked over and handed the phone to Cara.

It was Ginny.

Epilogue

No one recognized Iris at the funeral. How could they, they had never met her. She finally got to see who Connie was and to see Cara's face. She had heard about them for years, and now she could put an image to their names.

She stood in the back watching them all, the people who were in Jake's life. She looked around and saw some young women there too. Maybe they were just friends? Maybe he had slept with all of them?

She was surprised that only Jake's sister Connie got up to say anything. Actually, it was just really to read a poem.

She wished she could have gotten up. She would have a lot to say!

Iris went back to her small apartment after the funeral. She didn't bother to take the black dress and heels off. She knew Jake loved that dress. It was the same one he grabbed at when they had sex on the rug in his living room.

She walked to her kitchen shelf where all her plants had started to bloom. She had brought some in for the winter from the garden at her mother's home on Long Island. She had Gladiolus, Dahlias and Caladiums. Her favorite was the one with the beautiful pink flowers and long slim leaves, her Nerium Oleander. She picked up the small watering can on the shelf, filled it with water and gently fed all the plants.

She sat down and thought about Jake. He had called last week to tell her he had been offered a new job and was going to Lake George to relax for several days before giving notice at Benton & Bowles. He told Iris he would still see her Saturday as previously planned. She felt very happy about that until he told her that they needed to talk. She knew what that meant.

Iris felt she was the ideal woman for Jake. Always understanding, flexible with any changes in plans. She even accepted her weekend night change. She knew he thought he fooled her by telling her he worked on the other weekend nights. She wasn't that stupid!

She knew there were other women. Of course, when he went on those New Year's trips away, he would be fooling around.

She wondered how many fell for his charms and his lies. She felt sorry for them. She remembered seeing that poor young brunette across from Jake's apartment building stare at them that one time several months ago. Iris made a point to kiss Jake with a long sensual kiss right there on the street to show that girl exactly who Jake loved. Iris remembered that the girl stood still watching them through many traffic light changes.

Iris thought how easy it was. She asked Jake to come to her apartment, which he almost never did, but she knew that if he planned to end their relationship, he might not want to talk to her at his place. If he was at her apartment, he could walk away, not her.

When Jake arrived, she tried to get him to bed for the last time, but he insisted on just relaxing with her. He had a glass of wine with dinner, not his usual vodka, and Iris prepared a small pasta dish of chicken with basil for him. They had a casual dinner and light conversation. After dinner Jake took Iris' hands and proceeded to tell her how he needed to work on himself and since he was starting a new job, he wanted to be on his own and not in a relationship. Iris said she understood, but hoped that they could stay friends. Jake seemed very happy with that.

Jake had brought tarts from a bakery down the street. With dessert she served herbal tea. He normally didn't drink tea after dinner, but she said this was made from an orange blossom herb that was known to help blood pressure. For the new healthier Jake, he agreed to drink it.

It hadn't taken very long to infuse the Oleander leaves in the water. All it required was boiling water, washing several leaves and then dropping them into the hot water. When the water cooled, she poured the liquid into a blue jar and placed it in a shady area of her kitchen. That was back in April, when he told Iris that he would see her only twice a month because he was so busy. Right!

The flavorless liquid was easy to add to the tea. She put a tablespoon of honey in the orange tea so the Oleander infused water would blend in. She knew not to use too much because she wanted it to be undetectable in case an autopsy was done. She also knew the poison would mimic a heart attack. She decided if it just made him sick, she would stop by his place and nurse him, bringing more tea. After all, they would still be friends. It turned out she gave him the perfect amount.

Iris sat at her kitchen table for a long time. Finally, she looked at her watch. She was running late. She looked at herself in the full-length mirror in her hallway before heading out. The dress and heels still looked perfect. It's amazing how versatile little black dresses are. They are perfect for both funerals and dates.

Then she walked out the door.

Acknowledgements

I want to thank all my friends for their support and encouragement. My son Cameron Barker for his great feedback, his thoughtful insights on my drafts and his great enthusiasm. My mother Lemina Cashel for always being my cheerleader. Gayle Dinerstein for being my inspiration. Most of all I'd like to thank my husband, Barry Lippman, who has always been my champion. His love and support made this all possible.

About the Author

I grew up in New York City. I became a fashion designer, and traveled extensively throughout my career. During my travels, I met many fascinating people who influenced my characters. I have always written, mostly for myself, but am passionate about finding the right word and getting it down, from my memoirish account of discovering my family home in Brittany, France, to short stories and profiles of people in my life. I am also passionate about LGBTQ, #MeToo, and Pro-Choice issues that I address through the characters in my novel.